THE
MISTRESSCLASS

Also by Michèle Roberts

A Piece of the Night
The Visitation
The Wild Girl
The Book of Mrs Noah
In the Red Kitchen
Daughters of the House
During Mother's Absence
Flesh and Blood
Impossible Saints
Fair Exchange
The Looking Glass
Playing Sardines

Non-Fiction

Food, Sex & God

Poetry

The Mirror of the Mother
Psyche and the Hurricane
All the Selves I Was

THE
MISTRESSCLASS

Michèle Roberts

LITTLE, BROWN

A *Little, Brown* Book

First published in Great Britain in 2003
by Little, Brown

Copyright © Michèle Roberts 2003

A CIP catalogue record for this book
is available from the British Library

ISBN 0 316 72550 1

Typeset in Garamond by M Rules
Printed and bound in Great Britain
by Clays Ltd, St Ives plc

Little, Brown
An imprint of
Time Warner Books UK
Brettenham House
Lancaster Place
London WC2E 7EN

www.TimeWarnerBooks.co.uk

for Penny Valentine

Acknowledgements

Thanks to Gillon Aitken and all at Gillon Aitken Associates. Thanks to all at Little, Brown and Virago and, in particular, to my editor Lennie Goodings. Special thanks to Sarah LeFanu and Jenny Newman.

PART ONE

PART ONE

It's over. It's finished. I told myself to obey you and never to write to you again. Witness my weakness, then, that after this long silence I dare to address you once more.

My dear master.

Just writing those familiar words makes me feel we have never been parted. The language that links us is an invisible, living cord. Not the banal phrases of everyday, that others use, but a secret poetry which joins us one to another, mind to mind and heart to heart. That knot of belonging has never been untied. If I were not connected to you by that cord then I should die. From your lips I learned our hidden language and at your side I practised it. Picking up my pen to write to you I re-engage with cherished words that have remained fresh and evergreen, that are for ever and indissolubly associated with you. At the risk of displeasing you I cannot deny myself this indulgence. Forgive me.

You used to correct my *devoirs* for me in red ink, do you remember? You pointed out my faults with severity, but I cherished every red mark your sharp nib scratched on my paper; you did not draw blood; I translated your fierceness, understood your critical words as caresses on my skin. I treasured every savage and satirical rebuke you scrawled in my margins. My poor compositions, draft after draft laboured over with such toil. What made them worthy at all in any way was the pains you took to make me improve.

You don't want to read *this* composition. I know that. I should not be writing to you at all.

I'll start again.

My dear sir. I trust you are in excellent health, and Madame Heger too. And the children, of course. Please pass on to them my best regards. I hope that the school continues to flourish, and that your own studying and researches go well.

You wretched hypocrite, Charlotte. That is not at all what you want to say. You meek, genteel pretender, babbling clichés and polite nothings.

I apologise. To you, for bothering you, and to myself for writing falsely.

Children speak the truth, don't they? Until they are taught manners and conventional morality and learn to lie. Emily never lied. She always spoke the truth. She was fearless. She looked me in the face and said exactly what she thought.

If my daughter had lived I'd have brought her up to be as truthful as Emily. But she died. For a long time afterwards I lost all connection with the world of the living: I pursued my daughter towards the land of the dead. I sojourned there for some substantial time, wandering in the darkness, seeking her. Finally I decided to return. Back to the ashy world.

If my girl had lived I'd have had to consider sending her to school. I'd have taught her myself, here at home in Haworth, for as long as possible, but sooner or later, once she was growing up, I'd have had to contemplate sending her away.

If I had a living, breathing daughter, and not just this memory of a dead child, should I send her abroad to boarding-school? To Brussels, for example? To a *pensionnat* such as yours? What do you think, my dear master? Would you welcome her? Would you welcome me if I brought her to you?

A change of climate might do me good. Our wet weather makes me depressed. It has rained ceaselessly for over a month. It is the wettest spring I can ever remember, but then I say that every year. The front garden is a pond. The grave-stones in the churchyard are sinking. Water carves a muddy track along the road from the moors above, swirls off to the sides and floods the ditches. It swerves past the parsonage wall, swishes over the thresholds of the cottages in the street below.

But why should I write to you about the weather in England, which, as I remember you were fond of asserting, must be the worst in Europe? Why should I bother you by writing to you at all? Oh, my dear master, it is because I cannot prevent myself. Try as I might to forbid my hand to do otherwise, it will insist on picking up my pen. Try as I will to refuse to allow my thoughts to dwell on you, my heart to fill with tender memories of you, I am betrayed by these traitorous enemies within my gates, these servants who will not do reason's bidding. Short of tying myself to a chair or locking myself inside a cupboard – well, my hands must move; they must touch, if they may not touch your cheek, then at least this pen that circles around but cannot openly spell out my forbidden, inexpressible wishes.

For that reason, of course, I shall never send you this letter. As far as you are concerned I shall remain dumb and dead, buried in my moorland village, lost to good works and church on Sundays and the care of my husband and father.

These duties ought to be enough to satisfy me, I know. But much as I love my husband and my father they are not the only companions I crave. I miss my friends. I miss talking openly to them in letters. Arthur is afraid, if I write honestly to friends, that I shall betray myself and him. People are gossips, he says: why reveal your intimate secrets to the world? He trusts neither me nor my friends. I am forbidden to write to any friend who will not promise to destroy my letters once she's read them.

If I could write another novel I might be happier. But something inside me has dried up. I've lost that passion which was formerly the core of my being. I have turned aside to become the pattern of a good wife. I spend my days visiting parishioners in need, copying out Arthur's sermons, darning flannel nightclothes, peeling potatoes, reading to Papa, helping Martha turn out the parlour. Don't misunderstand me: I know these are honourable tasks, to be gladly embraced for the sake of the family I love and seek to serve.

Emily did not despise housework. She wrote at the same time. She kneaded bread while reading a book or composed in her head while doing the ironing. She cut out her own space for writing wherever she was; so powerful was her will that she pushed others to the distance she required. She carved a house of air and lived tranquilly inside it, and the rest of us were shut out beyond her invisible walls, watching her lips move as she peeled apples for the boiled pudding for dinner and made up poems in her head. I'm not like Emily. But it is not the fault of brooms and mops and colanders that I write no more. No, it's as though I cannot allow myself to believe now that writing should form the main activity of my life. I've lost the habit and the need and the desire.

Do you know why? Because you are not close to me any more, to inspire me and argue with me and spur me on.

I should like to go back to school, and learn how to write again. I should like to sit in your classroom, Monsieur, and learn from you. Had she lived, my daughter would need to go to school. How much more does her mother need some education!

My husband Arthur, who is a good man, I assure you, Monsieur, believes that a married woman can easily find time to write. That he never interrupts me or calls me away from my desk with some request. And since I'm sitting there writing nothing at all I let him summon me to come out for a walk or whatever else he suggests. Living with Arthur I can never be at peace for long because he works at home. He writes sermons in the study but he doesn't stay in there. Why should he? Now that we're married he's no longer the shy curate who lingers in the passage. The whole of the parsonage is his domain. He scatters his papers all over the dining-room; he prowls through the parlour searching for his pipe; he rummages in the bedroom for a clean collar. There's no corner which is safe from him. But it's not his fault I have gone dry.

He says of novel-writing that my words just flow on to the page. A leak, a spillage, like blood? He does not like to spell out his meanings. This is a house in which unspoken and unwritten words fly about trapped like moths at night attracted by lit lamps, rattling and bumping in the small rooms, my cramped heart, blundering at mirrors, trying to find a way out again. Words in this house pile up in corners, lie in heaps under the stairs, fall out of closets when you open them. Angry words are forbidden in a Christian house and so they have to be got rid of like dust and dirt. That's my job now: to throw words away; to control them and hold them down, like children weeping or like lunatics; to cover them with clean surfaces like the holland covers for chairs, the starched tablecloths for Sunday tea. But I am bursting with words, Monsieur; I have not changed from the girl I was when first you knew me; you encouraged me to speak, Monsieur, as you encouraged me to write; you listened to what I said and you read what I wrote and you responded to both.

How could I not love you? How could I possibly stop loving you?

I fell in love with you and longed to bear your child. A wicked wish. I was punished for it. I was driven away.

Of course I can't write another novel. Writing leads me to

daydream, to think of you. To imagine entering the room in which you are sitting reading. I approach you, taking your hand as you take mine. You address me kindly and you kiss me on both cheeks.

Then we begin to talk.

I planned to name my daughter Constantine, after you. Of course I did.

I shall tear this up. I shan't send it. But I have relieved my heart of its burden of words, and so I bid you good night, dear master.

I remain your ever faithful pupil

Charlotte

PART TWO

Perhaps it was a log, that dark shape, half submerged, propelled by the current from the direction of Blackfriars. Nobody except Adam took much notice. He spotted it because he was leaning over the western side of Southwark Bridge watching the play of sunlight on the choppy water below; mackerel patterns of silvery-black. Now a new motif entered the picture, disturbing the ripple dance.

Bulky and anonymous as a lost kitbag, the chunk of wood swayed along, floating gradually downstream, bobbing up and back in the wake of a passing launch. Finally it bumped against the raft supporting the group of engineers in white overalls and hard hats studying the profile of the Millennium Bridge. Above them, suspended on wires from the structure's underside, dangled little bales of hay, neatly trussed. Tourists on the far bank of the river, outside the Globe, chattered and pointed. Were these grassy cubes in fact sculptures, related to some *arte povera* installation at the nearby Tate? Were they a sophisticated means of testing and judging wobble and sway? Adam opted for recognising them as simple signs, to water traffic, of work in progress. He peered over the parapet, the sun in his eyes, as the log, or kitbag, came to rest in a swirl of straw and twigs. Something odd there. But squinting at it from this distance he could not say what.

Just west of Southwark Bridge, on the northern shore of the Thames at Queenhythe, the earliest Roman dock in the City is still clearly marked: a small oblong inlet, surrounded on three sides by modern flats and office blocks, with a walkway, fringing them, built out over the water on wooden stilts. At high tide the brimming river surges in and laps at these piles of stone and brick, rocking to and fro between their containing arms, slapping up against green slime. At low tide, when the flood retreats, a little beach appears, strewn with bits and pieces of debris tossed from pleasure-boats and carried along by the current until they catch and loiter here, a thick line of tarry dirt like a rim of scum on the side of an emptying bath. Plastic bottles, sodden cigarette packets, split footballs, lumps of driftwood: they wash up; halt; stopped in shingly mud. Further out towards midstream the moored Corporation rubbish-barge bears a sign request-ing crews and passengers not to drop litter; but they do. Let the river carry it all away: beer-cans, cardboard boxes, crisps packets, sandwich crusts; over the side with it, and away it swims; out of sight and forgotten.

Who was that woman walking to and fro down there, across the mud and stones? The sun dazzled on her red hair.

Vinny had driven to Waterloo with the effigy propped up next to her on the front seat of the van. Fellow drivers, stuck in neighbouring lanes at red lights or creeping past around packed roundabouts, took no notice of her odd passenger. When they hooted at her or gestured obscenely or deliberately nudged too close it was not because she had chosen to take a life-sized doll for an airing but because she was not aggressive enough in leaping through gaps or getting away from green lights and so was holding them up.

The effigy was constructed on the model of those guys she and Catherine had made every year, in childhood, for Bonfire Night. Nowadays children did not go to much trouble to make a Guy Fawkes. Collecting money was all that mattered. Penny for the old guy, Miss! Penny for the old guy! A pillowcase stuffed with a cushion, a balloon attached, was considered sufficient. But Vinny's guys had had faces and hats, arms and legs, and clutched handfuls of rockets. In my young day, she heard herself remarking fogyishly to the penny-collectors: we made proper guys. They would look at her patiently. Crusty old bat to be tolerated. Then she would give them fifty pence. She too loved fireworks.

The art competition was designed to garner publicity for the forthcoming weekend community festival on the South Bank. On the theme of heroes, it was open to London residents, of any age, working in any medium. Entries were to be delivered on Friday, ready for judging on Saturday morning, when the festival would be launched with a breakfast picnic and brass-band concert. Vinny was a poet, rather than a maker of soft sculptures. She decided to take part on a whim, just for fun. Working at the hospice, you grabbed any available chance to be childish and silly off-duty. She constructed the figure at night, when she arrived home in need of winding down. She finished it on the last evening of her temporary residency among the dying patients. She formed the torso and limbs from cotton bags stuffed with old tights. Tied the arms and legs in the middle, like joined sausages in a twisted skin, to make them seem jointed. The head was another bag, adorned with a wig of curled brown locks, and a papier-mâché mask, mouth agape, tied on for face. She dressed the figure in a frilled chemise and long lace-edged drawers from a stall in Portobello, two layers of ruffled petticoats, a long blue and brown check skirt and matching blouse, stockings, black lace mittens, a small bonnet, a pair of boots.

Once she had parked the van, she lifted the figure out, and strolled with it, her arm around its waist, towards the South Bank. She and Freddy had walked like that often, before Freddy had slid away three months ago and not come back. The wound closed over. Vinny stitched it up with strong black threads: strings of words for loss; glasses of wine; outings with friends. She wasn't heartbroken. No point pretending. Freddy had given her a good time, and then he'd gone away to give a good time to someone else.

A gang of teenage boys idled towards her, some with skateboards under their arms. Lumbered past. Spotting Vinny's companion, they turned back, clattered over for a closer look. Baggy trousers, big parkas with the hoods turned up. Trying to look fierce. Wanting her to feel threatened. To Vinny they looked like rebel angels. She smiled at them and said hello. Wrong move. She'd humiliated them by not showing fear. They surrounded her, mocking and jeering. They snatched the figure from her and ran away. She followed, calling at them to stop. They were tossing the figure from hand to hand, whooping and shouting because it was so light, so easy to throw. They were tearing off the blouse and skirt, the petticoats, the bonnet, rolling them up to make a football bundle, kicking it to and fro. She watched them chuck the figure into the water. They threw the clothes in, then the boots. The current swirled the effigy out into the middle of the river. Off it bobbed downstream, towards Blackfriars Bridge.

Vinny yelled curses. The boys laughed, dancing about just out of reach. Then she stopped shouting. Why be so upset? The whole thing had just been a game, after all. What had happened had happened. Call it a performance piece. Call it a day.

But she couldn't relinquish the game. It was not over yet. She decided to follow the effigy's progress. She sped north over Waterloo Bridge and began walking east on the broad pavement path under the plane trees. She passed the benches she loved, their armrests curled over black cast-iron crouching camels and sphinxes, the barges and boats turned into restaurants, Cleopatra's Needle, the war memorials and plaques to dead fighters and philanthropists. The half-sunken figure bobbed along just in front, on her right, and she went after it. Under Blackfriars Bridge and on to the walkway planted with ornamental vines and shrubs. Then, at the Millennium Bridge, the figure got stuck against a raft of men who seemed to be engineers. They wore bulky white overalls and clutched clipboards. The sun reflected off their white helmets.

Vinny perched on the balustrade fronting the riverside aspect of the Vintners' Building and smoked a cigarette, holding herself balanced with one hand. She swung her legs, gently beating the heels of her boots against the iron struts underneath her. Waiting to see what would happen next. To Adam, idly glancing down, she looked like any happy-go-lucky and idle tourist, dithering in the spring sunshine while she decided where to go. The Globe, or Tate Modern at Bankside, or along to the shopping at Butlers Wharf.

She glanced up, but, by the time recognition hit, he had turned away. But it was Adam. No possible mistake. She stared at him. High above her, he moved slowly forward on to the bridge, a tall shape in a big overcoat, broad shoulders hunched against the wind. Vinny jumped from her perch, crushed her cigarette underfoot, put the stub into her jacket pocket. She walked a little further along the riverside path, into the dock enclosure. Here she climbed up on to the restraining wall, swung her legs over, and clambered down the iron ladder strapped to the far side. The rods forming the rungs, striking up through her soles, hurt the arches of her feet. She winced, avoided the lowest three steps, jumped down on to the beach, the black rampart of mess.

Beyond the tideline was the tumbling river. Adam, a dark

silhouette, launched out over the water, had paused in the middle of the bridge to look at the view, to gaze down at the swirling tide.

Vinny's boots scuffed the squidgy sand. She picked her way back and forth among the mounds of anonymous waste as delicately as a wading bird. Stink of rot, whiffs of salty freshness, engine oil. The smell of the Thames as it ebbed strongly away. The north and eastern horizons prickled with tower blocks and church spires, glittering in the clear golden light. Above her the enormous spring sky leaped up and out, a dome of blue enclosing the smaller white dome of St Paul's.

The wind ruffled the surface of the river, scoured her cheeks, and a sudden cloud obscured the sun, darkening the water. Her neck felt cold. She fished in the pocket of her padded pink silk jacket and pulled out a red woollen scarf. She folded it in half lengthwise, wound it around herself, flipped the ends through the loop, pulled it tight. The sun dashed back out again, and she blinked.

She glanced over at the Millennium Bridge. The effigy lurched in the water there. She peered across at it.

Adam caught the gesture, the blur of pink as Vinny turned, the streak of red whipping out below him on the strip of beach. Robert had taught him, while he was still a child, to look at paintings as patterns, to let a figurative landscape dissolve towards abstraction, gestures of colour, that slithering-squeaking train clanking into Cannon Street behind him the excuse for a long, exuberant run of silver, the dancing water below the piers of the bridge an exercise in violet shadows. Robert would have been intrigued by this woman beachcombing among the rubbish far below. He would have appreciated her good clash of red and pink, the abandoned oar lying just behind her, the cairn of greasy-looking stones she kicked at with one booted foot. Her tufted hair was dyed henna-red. Twisted into cornrows, it stuck up brightly, the tiny plaits and knots sparkling above her velvet collar. Urban fox on the prowl.

He turned to look at the frieze of seagulls lining the parapet to his left. How big they were close up, and how sharp their beaks. Scavengers hungry for food. All of a sudden they flapped and rose, screaming, winged off over his head to hunt upstream.

He leaned over the parapet. The woman was trying to attract his attention. She looked just like Vinny. It was Vinny. She was waving at him. She was pointing at the shining arc of the Millennium Bridge, then at the raft beneath. The white-overalled engineers had clustered together, scrutinising the waves chuckling around them. The log floated close by. Half sunken. Matted with seaweed at one end. Hair. Human hair. One man took out a mobile phone, punched in a number. He shouted something. His words were carried away like gulls on the back of the wind.

The hand smoothed her forehead. The little rubber hose directed a flow of warm water over her temples. At the first touch of wetness Catherine closed her eyes.

– Not too hot, is it?

20

– No, it's just right.

Next came a cold handful of shampoo smelling of strawberries, tart and clean. Soapiness rubbed on. Nothing to do but abandon herself. Like being a child again, sitting in the bath opposite Vinny, having their tangled curls washed by their mother. Concentrated; eyes shut and knees up; not wanting it to end. To please her daughters Mum gave them a big soapy spike each on top. Jenny's fingertips, brisk and gentle as Mum's, began to knead her scalp, massage away the tiredness and tension of the working week.

Catherine's hair felt light, frothed up into a mousse of fruit. Feet planted on the floor, body swathed in smooth nylon gown, cool water hosing her scalp, swishing over her forehead and rinsing her ears, china edge of the wash-basin hard against the back of her neck, she was in someone else's hands. Forced to be passive for once; to let go of all responsibility. Basking. Arching her neck so that the sweet-smelling shampoo didn't get into her eyes, she laced her hands together over her stomach under her black tent, soothed by the burble of the radio and the women's chatter humming all around. Sometimes a squawk or a burst of laughter. They were screeching at each other's jokes. The jokes were about being single mothers and having no time for sex. About men who fucked and ran. About a girl they all knew who was fucking too many men at once. At first Catherine strained to listen. Then she gave up. A box of perfumes, this shop, stuffy and warm; you could just drift off and fall asleep.

Sharper pleasures that tickled you awake arrived once

you'd been swaddled in towels on top of your enveloping black gown, hair rubbed half dry; you'd been placed in the black leather chair solemnly looking at your reflection in the big mirror, feet tucked up on the metal rung. You closed your eyes once more. The comb glided through your damp rat-tails, flicking them to sleekness over and over again, and the cold metal of the scissors stroked the back of your neck. Shivering all over your skin, warmth building inside, all up and down your spine, fizzing, runny and sweet. Jenny just carried on clipping and trimming, intent on the ends of your hair she'd raised, gripped between her first two fingers, peered at as she approached them with her shining blades. Eyes narrowed and lips pursed.

Catherine smiled the same smile as all the other comforted clients in the salon and Jenny was pleased and handed her the mirror so she could check the sides. She'd had her long locks coloured back to the original red-gold, so that all the grey was gone. Adam always teased her about how much her hair-dressing cost, what with the highlights and the special conditioner and the manicure she had while waiting for the tints to take. He said he liked her grey hair so why hide it? He teased her about her face lotions too. What was wrong with a few laughter-lines? Catherine took no notice and went on spending her money on small, pricy pots of anti-wrinkle cream packed with miracle ingredients. Each pale unguent promised transformation. She tried them out, one after another. She was not ready to accept middle-age. She noted the freshness of young girls' skin with a pang. Whereas Vinny hooted at spending so much money on cosmetics and just slapped on Nivea Creme. She said it was like pasting plaster into cracks. But she'd always had oilier skin, and was now quite plump, which meant fewer wrinkles as she aged. She looked somewhat younger than fifty-two. But Catherine, at fifty-three, had better legs and hair, a better figure. These days you didn't have to give up, decline into blue rinses, middle-age spread. Catherine exercised. She dieted. She drank very little alcohol. She tried to get plenty of sleep.

– Your boys all right, are they? Jenny asked.

– They've gone travelling together, Catherine said: one's in his gap year and the other's taking a year out. They went off and got jobs and now they've gone to India.

– Oh, very nice, Jenny said: bet you miss them, though, don't you?

– It breaks my heart, Catherine said: but of course I don't let them know.

– I'm lucky, Jenny said: I've got my mum living just round the corner.

Reluctantly Catherine left cosseting behind and stepped out of the salon into the narrow street. She fastened the snappers on her lean white puffa coat. The neck and wrists were fringed with white fur. The coat was Italian. Very expensive. She had written an extra novella to pay for it. Porn, really, but aimed at women and so called erotica. All she had to do was keep on thinking up new ways of combining fucking with being hurt. *Crown of Spikes* had paid for her haircut. *Madame Punishment* had bought her shoes. The wind whipped her hair into her eyes and she put up her hands to catch it back. She jiggled from foot to foot to keep warm.

The little tunnel of shops cut east–west. The dome of St Paul's glimmered, fat and white, at one end. The hubbub of traffic rose up from the invisible main thoroughfares, the rumble of Cheapside to the north beyond St Mary-le-Bow, and, to the south, the surge of buses and cars at Mansion House just behind the tall buildings towering over her. There was a grind and clatter of roadworks. From a coffee-shop at the corner billowed the warm scent of baking bread.

Catherine hovered on the narrow pavement. She touched the mobile in her pocket. Where was Adam? Should she ring him? She was blocking the way. Passers-by scowled, stepped round her impatiently. Motorbikes were parked all along the kerb, and a couple of white vans, half on and half off. She was hemmed in by vehicles.

Here he came, loping towards her from the direction of Bow Lane, turning to glance at someone behind him. She was in a hurry, whoever it was. Turning her face away. A red-head in a pink jacket. She darted back the way they'd come, swerved aside into an alley. Seen from behind she looked uncannily like Catherine's sister Vinny. But Vinny was in France visiting her farmer friends Jeanne and Lucien, taking a break after finishing her job at the hospice. At this very minute she'd most likely be clumping around their vegetable garden in her wellingtons, deciding what to pick for lunch. Or, knowing Vinny, opening a bottle of wine and pouring herself an aperitif.

24

Adam stepped forward, blocking Catherine's view. He kissed her cheek.

– Sorry I'm late. You look lovely. Right, let's go.

He seized her arm, drew her forward, began to steer her across the street. She shook off his hand.

– Don't push me.

He marched ahead. Catherine increased her pace. This was just like being a child again, stumbling along on short legs: wait for me!

They reached the end of the street and turned south, towards the river. Catherine, trying to keep up with Adam, bumped awkwardly at his side. It was difficult to walk abreast on the crowded pavement. She dodged on and off the kerb, around parked cars, bollards.

– Let's have a drink in that pub in Borough Market, Adam said: the Wheatsheaf. Then I'll go to the gallery afterwards.

– You mean you haven't been to the gallery yet? Catherine asked: what have you been doing all morning, for heaven's sake?

Adam increased his speed. She put her hand on his sleeve to slow him down. He turned his face towards her. He shouted above the din of the traffic.

– Watching a corpse being fished up out of the river, if you must know.

The story took up a paragraph in the paper the following morning, tucked away at the bottom of a column on the inside page, a space reserved each Saturday for whimsical items of arts news. A foolish joke, the journalist opined, probably linked to the community arts festival on the South Bank that had opened that morning. A crude and meaningless rag: a ringleted effigy of the poet Shelley, costumed in trademark frilled shirt and pantaloons, launched from the shoreside at Waterloo.

Catherine folded the paper open and passed it to Adam as they sat in the yellow-walled kitchen eating breakfast. He read it, half smiling and half shrugging.

– What's so funny? Catherine asked.

– It stopped me getting to work on time, that's for sure, Adam said.

He swilled down his coffee.

– I promised Charlie to come in this morning, finish putting up the plasterboard. Then I'll be ready to start building the storage cabinets on Monday.

– You haven't forgotten the party tonight, have you? Catherine asked.

– I wish you'd never thought of it, Adam said: I'm not in the mood for a housewarming.

– Too late now, Catherine said.

He pushed aside the scrambled eggs she had made for him, pulled out a packet of cigarettes, and lit one.

– I know, I know, he said: I'm supposed to be stopping smoking. You don't have to tell me.

– So why are you smoking, then? Catherine asked: is something the matter?

26

– No, he said: I'll see you later.

He got up, kissed her cheek, and went out. She heard the front door slam. She looked at the congealed yellowy bulk of scrambled eggs on his plate, the crispbread crumbs on her own. She seized his dish, swapped it for hers, shovelled up his cold, grainy curds while finishing reading the paper. The arts festival promised world music from live bands, dancing, African and Caribbean food, an art competition, outdoor sculptures and theatre, an exhibition of banners, craft stalls. I'll go tomorrow, Catherine thought.

Her teaching notes, books and laptop occupied one end of the kitchen table. She scrabbled for pen and paper and wrote a shopping list. Taramasalata, olives, salami, crisps, peanuts, hummus, breadsticks, cheese. She cleared away the breakfast things, put dirty laundry into the washing-machine, swept the kitchen floor, hoovered and tidied the sitting-room. Then she went upstairs to sort through Robert's shoes and clothes. These were still in one of the cupboards in what had been his bedroom, which she now shared with Adam. The room in which they had slept at first had become Adam's study. Robert's house was small. No space for the boys when they returned from India. If they wanted to stay the night they'd have to sleep on the sitting-room floor. Catherine had redecorated the house from top to bottom after Robert's death. Now it gleamed – salmon and yellow and white and pale green.

She and Adam had brought Robert's suitcase back from the hospice. Adam had unpacked it and stored the contents away as though his father were coming home. A gesture of deference that Catherine understood. It was like keeping someone's name and telephone number in your address-book for a while longer. Too brutal to cross them out straight away. A betrayal of love. Cancelled. Gone. But three months had passed. A decent interval. Adam was not going to want his father's underwear, pyjamas, shaving-tackle. Nor his shirts. She threw all these things into a black plastic bin-liner. She added in the two good suits from the cupboard. She found herself sniffing as she worked. Stuffing a pile of vests into the sack, she whispered: sorry. The empty cupboard growled back at her. She slammed shut the gaping door.

She found, on leaving the house with her bulky bag, that someone had stolen some branches of lilac out of the front garden, just tearing them off and leaving the bush all ragged. She had been meaning to pick the lilac herself; they needed some flowers for the party that evening; and now there were hardly any blossoms left. So that sent her off, after her trip to the charity shop, to the florist's on Holloway Road.

She hesitated between the dark blue, almost indigo petals of anemones, flaring open around their fat, stubby hearts of black fur, and the paler blue clusters of hyacinths, their waxy curls. The packed bunches of flowers thrust up from silvery buckets set on metal stands jostled together on the wet concrete floor. The hyacinths' stems were so juicy and thick that the florist had tied them together in threes to stop them toppling.

Prodigal to buy cut hyacinths, rather than plant them at

home yourself in pots, but she had done no planting of bulbs last autumn. The world had shrunk like a collapsed balloon, air hissing out; it had shrivelled down to one small house, tired out; then to one upstairs room; finally to one bed in the local hospice. Flat, because Adam's father was so wasted and thin at the end that he hardly disturbed the blankets. Army-neat. His marigold pyjamas were too gay. He endured mostly in silence. Catherine thought the morphine dose too low but he wouldn't say. Remained as gallant as ever. When she and the nurse turned him, or lifted him higher up in bed from where he'd slipped down, light as a withered leaf, he would whisper: thanks, darlings. Such a big man become so little. Such a loud man become so soft.

The gang of artists attended the cremation at Golders Green. Old, faithful friends who had known Robert for forty years or more. Creased, battered faces. Paunches. Thinning hair. They all wore black; their habitual colour. Robert's was an atheist's funeral, with rock music and poetry. Nobody cried; as though atheists had managed to do away with grief as well as God. Catherine, who had retained some of the beliefs of her Catholic childhood, said secret prayers under her breath. The mourners held small white candles during the service, and afterwards left them, standing upright, still burning, on the stone floor of the little yard outside. White wands massed in a corner, stuck into puddles of wax to keep them steady. The candles did the weeping for the stiff, dry-eyed mourners. Solid grease softened into tears, pooled down, wet and translucent, then opaque. Mid-February.

Snow whirled from the grey sky, drifted against the cellophane-wrapped bouquets laid out in rows on the crematorium's redbrick patio. Forced narcissi and daffodils sparkled amid snow crystals. Now it was May, and today it was not raining, and the florist's shop brimmed with feathery greenery, spilled over with sweet-smelling blooms, and she had an excuse to buy some. Thanks to the lilac thief.

Catherine glimpsed a face. Outside the shop; peeping in. Fleeting image, like a snowflake. Precise, then melting. Framed by flowers, behind the glass. Like that image in *Orlando*: the beautiful dead woman preserved in winter as though in springtime freshness; haloed in blossoms; glimmering under the ice of the frozen Thames. Like that effigy Adam had seen yesterday; that he and the engineers had been convinced, for some moments, was a dead body. You were thinking of Robert, darling, weren't you? Catherine had said. Adam had downed his pint and begun talking of something else.

Catherine became aware of the face because the light changed. The shop flushed with warmth, as the sun skidded from behind a cloud and struck through the wide front window. The scent of the hyacinths gushed up like honey. The hyacinth as cosh, taking you by surprise. Clenched fists of colour and smell, that knocked you out. The face hung at the edge of her vision. She didn't notice it at first because she was concentrating on the flowers.

Niggers, anemones used to be called, Adam had told her once. Because, in mixed bunches, their black centres were surrounded by scarlet and purple and pink petals, the colours of the striped breeches worn by black slaves. A white person's term. The old boy who kept the flower shop near Brixton tube would holler to his assistant: fetch some more niggers from out the back! Some of the boys' white friends at school had insisted nigger was an ironic label and therefore cool. Vinny used to argue with them about it.

Would they have called Mrs Rochester a nigger? Poor Mrs Rochester: designated mad because she was too sexy, too fond of a drink, and a Creole. Catherine was teaching *Jane Eyre* this term, in tandem with *Wide Sargasso Sea*. They fitted together, like two parts of one mind. *Jane Eyre* was one of Vinny's favourite novels. *Wide Sargasso Sea* another. Both so hot and emotional. Catherine always found it a relief to get on to Henry James. Odd how she kept thinking of Vinny. Lucky Vinny, idling about in Jeanne's garden in France. She wasn't tied down to a regular job. She could take off there at a moment's notice. She could lie on the grass in the sun all day, doing nothing, if she so chose. But on the other hand she had no money, no house of her own, no husband and no children. She just drifted.

The florist was hovering nearby, waiting to pluck up the bunches Catherine pointed out. Niftily, with deft fingers, to pinch out the chosen ones without bruising the others. She was short and barrel-shaped, with a faded orange coiffure. She called you hen. Like her daughter, the manageress, she wore a pink nylon overall and black rubber boots. When she forgot what tulips cost today, or whether they'd had any lilies in earlier, she shouted for her daughter, Rochelle, Rochelle, and Rochelle would lounge out from the storeroom at the back where she made up the showy wreaths that locals liked to send for funerals.

The funeral parlour was just along the street. You'd see its Victorian-style hearse, the top-hatted and frock-coated driver in sable black twirling his whip over his team of black-plumed horses, heaving along Holloway Road up towards Highgate cemetery. The lofty entrance there, Adam had told Catherine once, was specially designed to allow the high-plumed horses to pass through. You could always recognise Rochelle's handi-work on the top of the hearse, elaborate sculpted artworks that spelt out Mum or were shaped like guitars or teddy bears. Adam thought such funerals were in poor taste. Catherine had had to convince him that it was all right to allow the mourners to send wreaths for his father, if they really wanted to. People of that generation liked sending flowers. Stupid, outdated symbol, Adam said. To the cremation he wore his red flannel shirt under his 1940s tweed overcoat, and no tie. He stood throughout the short service, tall and bony, with his hands in his pockets. His brown curls were greying. Did he look like his father? Yes. The boys didn't. They had round faces and snub noses and freckles; skin like hers, that burned easily. She'd packed them off to India with economy-size con-tainers of factor-25 suncream. Oh Mum do stop fussing.

– Settling in all right, are you? the florist asked: it's a nice neighbourhood, this, when you get to know it. Friendly. Very mixed, of course. But it takes all sorts, I always say.

The face glimmered at the window. A woman pressing close to the glass to peer inside. Her eyes were narrowed, her wide mouth set in a curve like a grimace. She had been there for some time, perhaps, when Catherine became properly aware of her, but equally she seemed to appear suddenly, like a waved white handkerchief flung up, held by one corner, flaring into the air. Then, even as Catherine turned and looked at her directly, she faded away; she withdrew and was gone.

On the counter, by the till, she spotted a paperback book. Its purple and black jacket shouted at her across the shop, as it was expressly designed to do.

– I'll take three bunches of anemones and three of hyacinths, please, she said.

The florist whipped the dripping bunches out of their buckets, spun them into paper sheaths she twisted into cones.

– Here you are then, hen, she sang out.

Catherine moved over to the counter. She glanced down at the paperback. Yes: one of hers. *Black Lace Handcuffs*, by Saffron Day. The heroine, tied up by the hero, gagged, then tenderly beaten, was thus cured of her frigidity.

– Oh, that's Rochelle's, said the florist: I don't read such nonsense.

She laid the wrapped flowers in her customer's arms. Catherine cradled them, waiting for her change, straining to see through the plate-glass door. The strange woman had vanished.

Leaving the florist's shop, she felt the cold wind whisk heat from her face. She dithered on the corner of Tufnell Park Road and Holloway Road, opposite the Odeon. This was the refuge to which Adam used to retreat in the after-noons, when he'd finished writing for the day but it was too early to nip out for a pint and he was bored. He lolled in the centre of the auditorium, surrounded by empty stretches of electric blue plush, hooked his legs over the seat in front, and watched films like *Terminator II*. He confessed his truancy to her when he came home, as though he expected a scolding. As though I'm some punishing mother, Catherine told him: when I'm not at all. Don't be so unfair. Adam was her darling, to be indulged. Two hours to herself. A couple of chapters' worth. She couldn't afford to take time off in the way that Adam did. Far too much to do.

At the start of this term Adam had given a public reading in the further-education institute where she taught literature part-time. Catherine organised the event. She put an announcement in the local paper; posted flyers around the neighbourhood; dragooned in her students. Adam was well known enough to attract a big audience. He talked to them about the carpentry and building job he'd taken up in April, made jokes about how bad he was at building walls. When one of Catherine's students, very serious, asked him: so why become a carpenter? Why didn't you get a job in a university teaching creative writing like other writers do? Adam replied: it's bad enough having to go out to work at all, but at least with this one I'm self-employed, I couldn't face a regular job. Everyone laughed, pleased with his honesty, except for Katy, the young woman who'd asked the question. She went red and looked furious. She came to evening classes since she was out at work all day. Obviously she supposed Adam was mocking people like herself who had what his generation called straight jobs. He didn't mean to, Catherine knew. It was just that he didn't want people to know he'd taken up the building job as part of his research for his new novel.

– Surely you know enough about building already? Catherine had asked: and what will you tell Charlie?

– Same as everyone else, Adam had replied.

Charlie, his employer, was an old school friend whom he'd recently re-met. Charlie had trained at art school, then gone into industrial design. Suddenly he'd thrown everything up and decided to open a gallery in the warehouse he'd bought years back as an investment. Adam was working for him six days a week.

Katy had a pointed chin and pale blue eyes. She was all in black. Catherine watched her push up to Adam afterwards, when he was seated at a small table by the bookstall, signing copies of his books. He'd looked up at her and smiled. Katy had given him one brief, intense look, murmured something, then turned away. There were girls like Katy hanging about at most literary readings. Skinny Pre-Raphaelite beauties in black velvet who wanted to be writers but didn't know how to write properly and hadn't the patience to learn, the patience for hard graft, years and years of it, and who thought that fucking writers was the next best thing. A kind of osmosis. Poetic acumen acquired by semen seepage.

Groupies, they were really. Adam was far too nice to them. He told them about writers' groups and poetry courses and creative-writing classes. He believed in helping the young. You mean you feel flattered by their attention, Catherine would say to him. Those wide-eyed little sweeties reminded her too much of herself and her friends when they were eighteen. Revelling in their youth and sexiness. Flirting with their male tutors at university as much as they dared. Wearing the briefest of mini-skirts to seminars; flashing plenty of bosom. It was a compliment if you were found pretty enough for a male academic to make a pass at you. Having an affair with the man who taught you gave you high status among your peers. Vinny, of course, hadn't seen it that way. Too fucking pure, Vinny was.

Catherine went to the Italian deli just up from the cinema and bought the party food. Holloway Road roared with traffic, stank with traffic fumes. She cannoned along it, head down. Once it had been a country thoroughfare, lined with high banks, down which sheep were driven to the market in Caledonian Road. Now the Victorian façades, above the garish plastic-fronted shops, were grimy and shabby. The pavements swirled with litter. As a newcomer to the district, she had relished its oddities: the funeral shop displaying headstones and marble angels, the fetish emporium full of black leather thigh-high boots, the scales and weights shop, the junk shops, the barber's unchanged since the 1950s, the Greek greengrocers selling small round aubergines, baby artichokes, prodigal bunches of rocket and coriander. But today, edgy, all she saw was a rubbish-strewn wasteland. She turned left and made towards Fleet Halt.

Adam was already back. He was lying on the sofa in the sitting-room, with the curtains drawn, smoking, the TV on, reading the paper by the light of a single lamp. Recently he'd taken to doing that. He said bright sunlight hurt his eyes.

She put down her bags of shopping and leaned against the doorpost. She wanted to tell him about the face that had appeared in the florist's window. Of course it must have been her own reflection, somehow distorted by the light on the glass. She opened her mouth then closed it. She presented him with the flowers. He put them down on the sofa beside him. She picked them up again and went off to find a couple of vases.

– Let's eat in here, OK? Adam shouted after her: I want to watch the end of the film.

The boxes of wine and beer for the party had been delivered while Catherine was out. She opened a bottle of white *vin de pays*, fished in the larder and fridge, laid out a platter of *antipasti*, a bowl of green salad, a basket of bread. She built a fire and lit it. After lunch she cleared away in the kitchen, then came back into the sitting-room and propped cushions against the sofa. She leaned back against them, legs stretched out, in front of the flames. Adam opened a second bottle of wine, poured himself a glass, gestured in her direction. Catherine shook her head.

– No thanks. I've still got plenty left.

He settled himself back full-length on the sofa.

– I bumped into Vinny yesterday, he said: by the way. Down by the river. I forgot to mention it, didn't I?

Catherine swallowed a cold mouthful faster than she had meant to. The wine hit her like green-gold fire along her veins.

– But she's in France, she said: at least I thought so. I'm sure she told me on the phone. I thought she was due to leave last week.

– She said she'd changed her mind and decided to stick around for a bit, Adam said: anyway, I invited her to the party tonight. It seemed like a nice idea. She said she hadn't seen you for ages. She hasn't seen this house, either. She said she'd like to see where we're living now.

His voice was casual. He turned on the TV and began flicking through the sports channels.

Catherine gulped down more wine. She kept her voice light and brisk, her face blank.

– Well, you've invited her, in any case. So that's that.

Adam was yawning over a boxing match. She seized the remote from him and turned down the sound. She pretended to doze.

PART THREE

Tonight, *cher* Monsieur, I've stayed up late to write to you. Papa is in bed asleep. Arthur is sealed away in his study with a hot toddy, composing this week's sermon. Rain lashes the window-panes. I've wheeled my work table close to the dying fire, for extra light. I've set a branch of candles just in front of me.

Having once begun to speak to you, having torn open the silence of years, I find I can't stop. I'd wrapped up my soul in silence, as you wrap woollens and store them away for next winter, against the moth; but now I've ripped myself open like an envelope and words are tumbling out.

Don't worry. I shan't embarrass you. I shan't send you this. It consoles me, that is all, to imagine that we may meet anew through this fleshless medium.

But why do I desire so ardently to see you again, *cher* Monsieur, when to be in your presence was such torture?

Here you sigh, lift your hand with that well-remembered gesture of impatience, reprove me for my ridiculous habit of exaggeration. Precision, my dear Charlotte, precision of expression, please.

Many times you explained to me that the artist must

indeed suffer, yes, perhaps to a degree that ordinary well-mannered well-meaning mortals, yes, like Madame Heger, might consider absurd, let alone tasteless and lacking in correct demeanour; but the heart of the message you expounded to me over and over again was that that suffering must be taken, held, ground in the crucible, reduced to fine dust in the heat of the fire. Then, only then, could something be made of it. When it was dry. When it was controlled, broken. When it was made into memory; transformed to gold by the power of alchemy; shaped at last into something bearable; finally into art.

You see I have remembered my lesson, Monsieur.

What else do I remember?

I remember that in the end it was indeed torture to be with you. A torture, however, to which I willingly, even eagerly, submitted myself. If pain were the price of seeing you, then so be it. It was a pain I relinquished with sadness, a pain that made me know I was alive, a pain I remember with actual fondness.

I remember, for example, that last occasion, just before I left for good, on which you invited me to come and eat supper with you and Madame Heger and the children. A Sunday privilege for the children; allowed to stay up; and for me too. All was as usual. The dining-room gleamed with cleanliness: the polished floor, the porcelain tureen on the sideboard, the brass pots of trailing ivies and ferns on the chiffonière, the biscuit ornaments and candlesticks on the shelf above the stove. The oval table was covered with a snowy cloth, and you presided at its head, your white shirt-points and neckcloth, stiff as the table napery, testifying to the housekeeping prowess of your wife who sat next to you smiling serenely. I was opposite her, and, as usual, I studied her beauty. She was not small and thin, like me, but well made; curved. Her mouth was soft and red, her cheeks plump. Glistening ringlets, bunched like black grapes, fell on her neck, her embroidered collar. Her eyes were large and dark. All her gestures were languorous, slow; and yet she was the undisputed ruler of the house. Of course she was: you loved her. Inside the house you gave way to her with energy and grace.

How calm the room. How calm you both seemed. Madame Heger controlled the children with sidelong glances, shakes of the head, the lift of a finger. That was always sufficient, given the threat of greater reprimand: being banished upstairs without cake or dessert, or, in cases of dire badness, being beaten. You kept the rod in your study, or rather Madame Heger did, hung behind the door; a lean little god. She didn't call it punishment; she called it teaching her darlings better; teaching them self-discipline; she whipped them into behaving beautifully at table; which mostly meant not speaking and not gobbling. I was like one of those children; yes of course I was. I yearned to remain in your presence, to please you in every possible way, and never to arouse your wrath.

You didn't need to use rods or whips or switches on your pupils in class. Your methods were to stun with satire, to draw blood with a single, well-aimed insult delivered with a smile, to drive us mad by praising us contemptuously.

You knew precisely how to make me suffer. All you had to do was avert your face. Speak to one of your other favourites. Ignore me. But at least it was your real face that you turned away.

Now you sat opposite me at the supper-table and asked me charming and courteous questions about my studies, my hopes for the future. You were cool and impersonal and I knew it was necessary; that you could not behave as you did when we were alone in the classroom or your study together, discoursing warmly, even passionately, on literature; but nonetheless I hated you.

A tornado blew up in your dining-room. You pretended not to notice. The tornado was in me. A magnetic force kept sucking me across the table. To glue me on to you. I was aware of every movement that you made, second by second, turning left and right to talk to Madame Heger or your oldest daughter (how I loathed that child with her lisped pieties and her corkscrew curls and her soft eyes beaming up at her *cher papa*; she was shameless, a tiny slut who already knew all the seductive arts and practised them on you every Sunday), inclining your head to listen, making them feel cherished and important. As of course they were. As they are.

I was pulled ruthlessly across the table towards you and had to lay my hands on the table edge to stop myself flying to you. I could not speak the words I wanted to. Terror of revealing my feelings kept me dumb and forced me into inane politenesses. Thank you so much, just a little sugar, yes, please, another slice of vanilla cake, some more of this delicious pear conserve. I knew I sounded stupid, insincere, inept, stumbling. I could see Madame Heger thought me as well behaved as usual; also a great gawk; a very dull person. A very correct *jeune fille* with her lips pinned shut saying nothing out of place. Oh, the boredom I must have caused her. I was her work of charity for the week, the young *assistante* so far from home: of course we must invite her, *chéri*. I couldn't bear her semblance of kindness: so brisk, so easily shrugged on and off. I wanted to scream, to hurl my cup of coffee against the pink-striped wallpaper, watch satisfied as brown liquid stained and splashed and she'd have to leap up with a loud cry and fetch the maid to get a cloth.

I could not be my true self with her in the room, Monsieur. It was not possible. It was not permitted.

There she sat, reasonable, cold, composed, pouring out coffee from the tall green porcelain pot, tilting the spout at exactly the right angle, never spilling a drop, and passing the thin gold-edged cups as though the room were not ablaze the table were not exploding with heat I were not rising up into the air screeching like a wounded demon with the pain of all I must repress in my heart. There she sat not knowing that behind her the blue damask curtains were on fire.

And then the next morning she insisted that she wanted to accompany me on the coach that would take me to the boat. Her duty, she conveyed: to see me off her premises.

Have mercy, Monsieur. I dare not ask you for what I want.

Yet you know it without my uttering a word. You read my begging thoughts, my pleading eyes, as expertly as you read your students' essays.

Correct me, chastise me, but don't blot me out completely. Show me how to do better next time.

Now I'll burn this.

Ever your

Charlotte

PART FOUR

Reader, I married him.

Vinny let *Jane Eyre* fall closed, the hardback cover coming down like a lid, and folded her hands across it. The copy she'd had since early adolescence, pages yellowing and dog-eared, end-papers spotted and foxed; given to her by her mother forty years before.

Box of words balanced on her stomach. She hugged the novel to her. She had been inside it, like Jonah swallowed by the whale in one convulsive gulp, but now held it separate from her. Two whales. Fin touching fin, swimming together in the sea of story. The book was a casing for something alive, made of the same stuff as herself. Entering it was stripping off to run into the water, returning to her true element. Words surrounding her, buoying her up.

She knew *Jane Eyre* almost by heart. Reading it was effortless, like floating rocked in salt waves just off a boulder-strewn coast. Opening the novel you kicked out through curling foam as the shingle dropped away and the blue-green depths opened up beneath you; then you turned on to your back and let the current carry you where it would. Also, reading *Jane Eyre* was like reaching land. Being tipped out from turquoise sea; beached; stumbling up a slope of silver-white sand towards a fringe of trees to find what lay beyond. Inhabiting a new country. Compelling; drawing you in. You vanished; dissolved. No ego left. That was the rapture: the self no longer existed. You were gone.

If you thought about reading you couldn't do it. The words ceased to be transparent, a web of little black stars, black shining connections, but stood up like metal lines of fences, knots of barbed wire, forbidding entry. What a bizarre activity, when you considered it: transformative like an act of magic, the brain rapidly translating arcane symbols into sounds and signs that it understood. A work of resurrection. Something flat and seemingly dead stood up and waved and sang. You could only read if you forgot you had a body located in time and space, if you allowed yourself to become transported. To that new place where you had never been before. A land of bliss. Yet at the same time it was the body that responded, shuddering all over at the pleasure given by the prose.

Reading was about being carried away. Just like falling in love for the first time all those years ago. Snatched up and taken elsewhere, like Persephone rapt by the king of the underworld; overpowered and carried off. But those philosophers she'd read in the late seventies had put it the wrong way. They said the pleasure of reading was like coming; a sexual thrill. But Vinny thought it could be the other way round: the pleasures of sex could trail the pleasures of reading. She'd loved reading way before she ever had sex. Reading

50

had been the primary rapture, the primary glow. Did that make her neurotic? That psychiatrist she'd had to see, all those years ago, when she was trying to get her abortion, would have thought so. He suggested Vinny had trouble engaging with what he called real life. Vinny loved the fantasy world too much, he said. Writing was all very well but. What was she doing, a healthy young woman in her mid-twenties, asking to abort a child? She should marry the father and get on with her life. She should be ashamed of herself.

Vinny rolled a joint, lit it and inhaled. Heady aromatic rush. She let out her breath in a sigh. Rapture of sex rapture of reading rapture of drugs. She leaned back. The room was warm. It smelt of dope and of the sprays of lilac she had stolen and brought home with her last night. Coming back late, walking slowly in the freshness after the spring rain, half tipsy, she had smelt the lilac blossoms in the darkness, the invisible tree heavy with sweetness, its full branches arching over evergreen hedges, catching her hair, touching her forehead as she stopped and looked up.

Loose pearls of water tilted down like blessings. A shower of dewy drops. She drank in the heady smell. Glimmer of whiteness. Irresistible. She reached out her hands and broke off the jigging branches, jerking more wetness on to her face. She encircled the flowers with her arms, tenderly and greedily, their cool cones of curled petals, then walked home holding them. Steady and stately, cradling her bouquet. Like a bride. Now the long sprays of lilac, green and white, filled her room with their powerful scent. Like the wafts of perfume drifting through the garden of Thornfield on that Midsummer's Eve; the walled, enclosed garden; paradise by moonlight; when Mr Rochester finally tells Jane he loves her.

Her mother had had little sympathy with Vinny's love of novels. She thought that reading was dangerous because it stirred you up and encouraged you to imagine things. All manner of falsity and wickedness. The imagination was a term her mother used to designate everything that was not true and that therefore caused trouble. Books made Vinny cry. They gave her ideas. Sometimes they gave her nightmares. The madwoman in the attic certainly had, first time around. If her mother caught Vinny reading in the afternoons at weekends, when all sensible children like Catherine ran about playing, she would snatch the book from her younger daughter's hands and pack her off outside. The nuns at school also thought books were dangerous, but for different reasons. Books brought you too much pleasure, they hinted, especially if you lay reading them on your bed before lunch. Books had to be measured out in doses, for education, but swig too deep in secret and their delicious nectar clouded your mind and corrupted your soul. Books were sex'n'-drugs'n'rock'n'roll. The nuns were at one with the philosophers about that. It's a mercy, Vinny thought, that between Mumma and the nuns I ever got any education at all. But, thanks to all those books she had devoured, she had got into university easily, no problem. There, you could lie in bed all day reading and call it work.

She took a long toke of her joint. That was the other

reward of reading. Books were inexhaustible. You ate them and drank them and, mysteriously, they renewed themselves. Magic bread and wine, like Holy Communion; oases in the desert; fountains that never ran dry.

She yawned. She was stretched out in the big armchair she had hauled in, up five flights of stairs, off the skip down the road. Her left foot was planted on the floor and her right leg slung over the arm, green leather mule tilting off her toes and swinging, just far enough that it did not fall off. The arm-chair was wide and deep, its sagging springs nailed back into place under two strips of wood. Four nails, four whacks with a hammer. She'd covered the chair with a couple of old cur-tains from a jumble sale, pinning on the worn blue and green chintz with heavy drawing-pins. She'd done two cushions to match.

The council flat was low-ceilinged and poky, but Vinny didn't care. The triumph was to have got a flat at all. Single people were not a priority on the waiting-list. It had taken ten years of queuing, persuading, complaining, haranguing, arguing. Finally, fifteen years ago, she'd done it. She'd acquired her own scarlet front door on the fifth floor. Riches. She even had a small metal-sided balcony she'd turned into a garden in the sky. A morning-glory, just in bud, rose from a pot and wreathed along the railings. Sweetpeas and clematis hooked green tendrils up the trellis on the back wall. The kitchen window-sill bore pots of herbs, a trough of gerani-ums. There was room for two canvas chairs, if she sat knee to knee with guests. The noise of cars seemed far away, muted.

You could look down over Seven Sisters Road or you could look up and watch aeroplanes go by.

Vinny had painted the walls of her two rooms turquoise and lime-green. Her bedroom was just big enough to hold a double bed, shelves for clothes and books. In the small sitting-room the armchair was her important place, because it was where she sat to do her reading and writing. You could curl up in it, or perch in it cross-legged. You could wheel it about, to face the window, or to approach the rickety little bamboo table, another skip treasure, where she kept her stash tin, cigarettes, and current pile of books. In the mornings she got up early, made coffee and toast in the galley kitchen, then returned to her armchair, to lounge, balancing her cup and saucer, sipping coffee and gazing out at the morning sky in the intervals of reading, or reworking a poem. A good day began that way, with enough time to slide from sleep to a silent breakfast, hunched and intent, beginning a new chapter of her book or a new piece of writing. After concentrating for an hour she was ready to go out to work. Poets had to have day jobs. Vinny took whatever she could find. She had enjoyed her part-time residency in the local hospice in which Robert had died. Perhaps it was in acknowledgement of that death, she thought, that she had made the effigy.

No time to wonder about that now. Five o'clock in the afternoon. She shook off her slippers and swung herself up out of the chair. The party began at eight. If the rain held off, she could walk there, rather than undertake the tortuous journey by bus and tube.

Adam and Catherine had moved months ago to Fleet Halt, between Holloway Road and Tufnell Park tube. Vinny had never yet visited them there. She'd looked up the street in the *A–Z*. A district, so close to her own, she didn't know well. A separate village. Though she'd strolled around it last night, on a whim, just to get a taste of it, in anticipation of arriving there the following day. Wanting to feel in control of the unknown. Promising herself she'd just dart through. Certainly she wouldn't go near their house. Though the address was imprinted on her memory. But she hadn't been able to help herself. She'd slowed down then circled back, retracing her steps along the street to stare at Adam's new home, a late-eighteenth-century cottage, small and low, one of several in a row squashed in between two mid-Victorian terraces.

She had let herself walk past the house just once, last night; she'd paused by the gate, summoned by the scent of the flowering lilac; she'd stolen a branch or two; then she'd darted away, almost running, in case Catherine came to the uncurtained window and spotted her. This morning, when she'd paused outside the Odeon on Holloway Road to check the new programme, she'd seen her sister go into the florist's shop, watched her choose an armful of flowers. Interesting, to study someone you knew well, when they weren't aware of you. Not spying, exactly. Vinny told herself she preferred to be the one who looked rather than the one who was looked at, that was all. And she knew so little about Catherine's life now. She had been waiting a long time for an invitation to visit Adam and Catherine in Robert's house, and at last it had come. She wanted to see what her sister would be like in that place. Usually they met in bars, for a quick drink. Nothing too intimate. Likewise, she went to an occasional exhibition with Adam. She rarely saw the two of them together. Threesomes were too difficult. Too painful. She wanted to go to their party but she felt nervous at the prospect. The dope began to ease through, and calmed her.

She rummaged through the clothes hung on the back of her bedroom door. She had hoarded three 1940s crêpe-de-Chine frocks bought from jumble sales in the late sixties; slithery; cut on the bias. She chose one in dark red. Knee-length, with square shoulders, a V-neck, elbow-length sleeves, and beading on the yoke. She put on sheer stockings, black wedge heels.

The walk from Seven Sisters Road and through Fleet Halt seemed endless tonight. Houses repeated and repeated, flashed up and past, made you feel you were dancing on the spot under strobe-lights. The weather changed while Vinny was *en route*, grew newly cold and rainy. She walked as fast as she dared in her rigid heels. Underfoot, cracked, uneven pavements, grouted with black tufts of weeds, tilted to trip her up. She kept an eye out for the dog turds toppled and smeared by the feet of previous passers-by. One anonymous row of bow-fronted façades gave way to another, front gardens dark and bedraggled in the rain. She bent her head against the wet and struggled on, the wind whipping at her clothes.

Number four was in the centre of the row of cottages, which were set back from the narrow street behind a row of tall black railings. Pushing open the gate, walking past the denuded lilac tree, up the flagged path, Vinny saw what she had not noticed last night: the long crack running up the brick front. Adam was working as a builder now. So why didn't he mend his house?

Catherine opened the front door. Colour and light and music rushed out from behind her. Vinny blinked. Her tall sister looked like the angel with the flaming sword guarding the entry to Paradise. She stood haloed in a gold glow, one hand on the doorknob. Then she smiled, and became human again.

– What a filthy night, Catherine cried: you must be soaked.

Vinny stumbled in. The tiny hall smelt clean and flowery. She halted, aware of mud and grit from outside brought in tracked across the pale carpet, her sodden jacket leaking. She peeped again at her sister. Catherine's long, red-gold hair framed her pale, oval face. She looked invincible. Like a warrior princess in her knee-length scarlet silk shift, which showed off her slender legs.

They kissed each other gently, putting their hands on each other's waists, brushing cheeks. Catherine was very slim. Scant flesh on her. Vinny felt she clutched a handful of bones.

– You've had your hair done, she said: you look lovely.

– So do you, Catherine said: that colour really suits you.

They eyed one another, half smiling. Ritual skirmish of swords over with. Bows and flourishes exchanged.

– Why didn't you tell me you were still in town? Catherine asked: why didn't you go straight off to France, as you said you were going to?

– There was this art competition I decided to enter, Vinny said: but then I lost my entry. It got stolen.

She wanted to tell Catherine about making the effigy, but she had chosen the wrong moment. Catherine was not interested. She interrupted.

– Come and leave your jacket, there are lots of towels if you want to dry your hair, in here, look.

Catherine's voice and hand whirled her into a cloakroom furnished with a washstand and dressing-table. Square gilt-framed mirror tipping forwards. Chintz-covered chair. Dark crimson walls thick with pictures.

– Then when you're ready come and join us through here and get a drink, Catherine went on: there's brushes and combs there. Help yourself to anything you need.

She whisked off, was gone. Vinny shook off her jacket and laid it on a heap of others, on the armchair. Then, realising how wet it was, she picked it up again and draped it across the sink. The room smelt of damp coats. Like the cloakroom at school, that dark, inviting place where you could hide on freezing November afternoons, pretending to have bad period pains in order to skip hockey. Their mother had always provided the requisite note. She had chosen an institution run by nuns because she thought that meant a better education, but she did not force her daughters to do sport they disliked. Oh, I do sympathise, darling. I remember at my grammar school we had to play hockey and netball in awful grey-flannel divided skirts. What Vinny remembered was not the game itself but the wind shaking the tops of the black elms, the red braid tied across her yellow Aertex shirt, her raw purple knees, her hurting breath on the way home, the studded boots clogged with mud, which she scraped clean outside the kitchen door, sitting on the step.

Robert's place did not look like a grey-flannel and hockey household. The paintings were pastiches of Matisse: smiling women in dressing-gowns reclining on *chaise-longues*. The cake of carnation soap smelt spicy and expensive. Even the clutter seemed festive. Briefcases and open carrier-bags of books were wedged together on the parquet floor. Umbrellas had been stuck in a bucket. Boots and shoes had been flung down here and there, lolled about in mismatched pairs.

Vinny took a fluffy blue towel from the pile on a little table and applied it to her face. She squirted on some eau-de-toilette from a bottle on the washstand and tweaked her hair into place.

She breathed deeply, to calm herself. Then she went back into the hall, plunging down it away from the front door, towards the back of the house and the party.

Originally the little house must have had two small rooms on the ground floor. The tiny hall and cloakroom had taken a slice off the front one, leaving the back one wider. The dividing wall had been knocked down, an archway built in its place. The room swung like a golden bell, tonguing out laughter, conversation, music, cigarette smoke. Vinny shimmied into it, around the edges of it, as though she were dancing. Floating in this pink-golden tent suspended between long windows black with rain; watching Catherine swivel past with a bottle under each arm, her white wrists encircled by gold bangles. That shiny badge on her left hand: gold wedding-ring. Firelight, glittering from the iron basket of burning logs in the white marble fireplace, reached out to the pale yellow wooden floor strewn with salmon rugs, to the lace blinds and the cream and white striped curtains, tied back with white cords finished with gold tassels, and was reflected in the mirror hung opposite. Still-lifes of fruit and flowers in gilt frames jostled each other on the pale pink satiny walls. Catherine had told her she'd done the place up. You should have seen it, Vin. A terrible tip. The refurbishment was opulent, even gaudy, Vinny thought. Like a boudoir. What on earth did Adam make of it?

Her eyes raked back and forth like spotlights, found Adam on the far side of the crowd. He stood out, just as he always had, as though he glowed in the dark and was eight feet tall. She began to inch towards him. He was carrying a tray of glasses and bottles and she needed a drink.

Catherine, hardly turning her head, watched Vinny wriggle through the pack of people, and smiled. Not very subtle, her little sister. Not just pretty, but determined too. Ferocious when necessary. That little one could bite. And I can bite back, Catherine thought. They might both be turned fifty but inside they were still teenagers, jostling and pushing, the older one forever chivvying the younger, the younger one forever trying to overtake the elder. As children they contained their struggles by playing at being dogs. Trotting and gambolling. Apparently casual. Ready to snap into snarling and pouncing; worrying their prey. Dogs make secret paths through gardens, run on hidden routes. Whistling through the grass, noses down, hunting. Next day you spot their flattened track, narrow, between the seed-laden stalks. Catherine was like that tonight. She followed her own tunnel between groups of her friends, clusters of her teaching colleagues, a scattering of neighbours. She was disguised as a good hostess going where she was needed, offering her guests canapés, topping up their glasses of wine, but she was scenting as keenly as any hound. One eye on Vinny and Adam. Her run took her back and forth near the door to the hall and so to the front door. Every so often she paused, ears pricked, alert and listening. When the bell sounded she could ease out of the crowd and go promptly to answer it.

Charlie arrived late. He plunged in, out of the rainy blue dusk, as though he were swimming. His black hair was plastered with wet. His turquoise eyes were brilliant and luminous, like sun on seawater. He was sleek as a seal, with a wide, curved smile.

– Catherine. How are you? You look great.

His arms reached out to hug her then flinched back. Don't get the wrong idea, he was saying: Adam's my good friend, my loyalty goes to him. But Catherine wanted him to play the game, admire her. She shouted in her head: why not flirt with me? She was still young enough to appreciate men's glances in the street, to want love and sex. Adam might have gone off sex but she hadn't. Charlie might not scowl like Mr Rochester but he would do. She wondered what he looked like with his clothes off.

Charlie leaned down and kissed her cheek. He was wearing black jeans and a black leather jacket over a black T-shirt. The neck of a bottle of wine, swathed in damp blue tissue paper, stuck out of one deep jacket pocket.

– Sorry I'm late. Phone calls. I've got the first few shows organised but there's still some loose ends to tie up.

– The work's on schedule, though, isn't it? Catherine asked: Adam said you're opening in six months' time?

– Sure. Just need to book a few more shows for next year and we're well away.

Charlie was having an unashamed good look round. His gaze swept over the paintings lining the walls.

– These are nice. Whose are they?

– They're all Robert's. Adam's father, Catherine said: this was his house. We moved in to look after him when he became very ill.

62

– Adam's father was a painter? He certainly kept that quiet when we were at school.

– You know what Adam's like, Catherine said: he doesn't talk much about himself.

– Shy bugger, isn't he? Charlie said: he's never mentioned it recently, either.

– The house is chock-a-block with Robert's paintings, Catherine said: we haven't got round to sorting them all out yet. I want to, but Adam's always telling me not to be in such a rush.

Charlie had his hands in his jeans pockets. He was leaning forward, his eyes narrowed with concentration. Getting as close to the paint as he could. Now he turned and looked at Catherine.

– Do you like it here? Where did you live before?

– We had a housing-association flat in Bethnal Green, Catherine said.

Adam's old flat, that he'd had since he was twenty-five. She had been a local in the shops. A regular in the pub. She had enjoyed knowing all the shopkeepers' names, chatting to them as she went in and out. People complained about the impersonality of cities, but that was only because they didn't bother shopping in small shops, spending two minutes talking to the assistants who served them. When she and Adam decided to move to Fleet Halt and give up the flat, she had gone round and said goodbye to everyone. Uprooting yourself, you didn't just leave a district, an urban landscape: you left local friends. She missed them. Mr and Mrs Patel in the paper shop. Mr Hassan in the dry-cleaner's. Jack and Alice Ritchie in the Mayflower. Now she was having to start that process of getting to know people all over again, and it felt as though she were being faithless to the ones she had known before.

– I don't know whether we'll stay here or not, she said: it all depends on whether Adam decides to sell this place. He'll have to fix it up a bit if he does.

She stretched out her hands to take the bottle Charlie was extracting from his pocket. Its coldness came through its dark blue wrapping on to her palms.

– Did you see that crack in the façade when you arrived? All the houses in this row need underpinning. The river Fleet runs bang underneath and they're all gradually sinking into it.

Charlie moved away from the front door, past the hat-stand. He surveyed the pair of paintings hung on the left-hand wall. French landscapes in oils. One showed a clump of red-roofed farmhouses in a green valley. The other depicted an orchard in blossom. The colours were bright, hot, non-naturalistic, the brushwork gestural.

– Safe, aren't they? Catherine said: nice, though.

– Mmm, Charlie said: competent, certainly.

Catherine came to stand next to him. She stared at the pictures.

– He trained at the Slade. He knew how to make work that would sell, all right. He made quite a bit of money. He ended up owning a house in France as well as this one.

– Where did he show? Charlie asked: what gallery was he with?

– He was with the Bretton for a long time, Catherine said: but he left them a couple of years ago, after a row over their percentage. He started having studio shows. Then he got ill, so that was that.

Charlie's face, intent, professional, gave nothing away. In that respect he was just like Adam. Mask held up whenever necessary.

– These seem a bit pot-boilerish to me, Catherine said.

– Maybe, Charlie agreed: I'd certainly like to see the others, though.

– Have a look round upstairs, Catherine said: in our bedroom, the room on the right. The best one's in there. So I think, anyway. I'll take you up there later, if you like.

She caught his gaze and smiled at him. She felt the smile wash across her face, a tide of warmth.

The doorbell pealed.

Charlie lifted a hand. He headed for the open door at the back of the hall, the hubbub of voices and music. Catherine let in more guests. She went into the kitchen to find the corkscrew, put a bottle of wine under each arm, then crossed the hall again and plunged back into the party. She worked her way across the room, greeting people, shouting above the din, towards Adam. He was talking to Vinny. She was standing close to him, twirling a wine glass by its stem.

– Charlotte Brontë? Adam was saying: you don't still like her, do you?

65

– You ought to give her a second chance, Vinny said: I suppose you think she's merely a woman novelist and so that's that. But you should read her. You might be pleasantly surprised.

She waved her glass. Wine leaped out and slopped on to the floor. Catherine grimaced, then quickly tried to look pleasant. Adam caught her eye and twitched the side of his mouth.

– And then, Vinny went on: we haven't only got the novels. We've got a record of her learning to write with Monsieur Heger. All her juvenilia's mad Gothic stuff, really wild and all over the place, but he taught her to write more plainly. More realistically.

Catherine swallowed a yawn. Adam shrugged very slightly.

– Go on, Vinny, Catherine said: you're dying to tell Adam. Who was Monsieur Heger? I know, but I bet he doesn't.

Vinny's words spilled out almost incoherently. She must be drunk.

– Her professor. Charlotte attended his school in Brussels with her sister Emily, and then the next year she went back on her own, as a teacher. She fell in love with Monsieur Heger without really realising what was happening. Once she'd left, Charlotte wrote these pleading letters to him, asking him to continue corresponding with her. Much too passionate. He stopped writing back, and forbade her to write to him any more. He tore up her letters and threw them in the bin and thought that was that. But his wife went through his wastepaper basket and found the letters and stitched them back together and secretly kept them. That's how we know how desperately Charlotte was in love. She broke her heart over Monsieur Heger and as a result was inspired to write her masterpiece.

Vinny eyed the bottles Catherine bore in her arms. Catherine took the hint and tipped out more drink. She felt as though she were a garage attendant, filling up long-haul lorries.

Vinny clutched her glass in one hand and a cigarette in the other. She wreathed herself in blue smoke and took quick, nervous sips of wine. The smell of fresh nicotine mingled with that of booze, perfume, and perspiration. Music thumped from the speaker in the corner behind them, and Vinny moved her hips to the beat, seemingly unconsciously, as Adam glanced back at her. She was twitching her hips in a bed dance; bump and grind. She was much too old to do that, Catherine thought. She ought to behave.

– I do sometimes wonder, Vinny continued: what would have happened if Charlotte hadn't died in early pregnancy. If Monsieur Heger had somehow come back into her life. Perhaps they would have had an affair after all.

– Charlie's here, Catherine said to Adam: he was over there, in the corner, a minute ago, but now I can't see him. Have you spoken to him yet?

Adam removed the wine bottles from Catherine.

– I'll circulate with these, and then I'll come and talk to Charlie.

Vinny slid between tightly wedged groups of chattering people towards the door. The other guests were rocks, whom she could flow past, easy as water, sinuous as a sea-serpent winding in and out behind people's backs, bending away from the tilting glasses clutched in their hands that waved like fronds of seaweed and splashed gold drops on to the glistening floor. Adam lolled in the far window-seat. She turned her back on him, glided out of the door, and into the hall.

The hubbub behind was sealed away. Cooler out here. From a hatstand hung a blue raincoat she hadn't noticed earlier. It must be Adam's. Those must be his boots. She shook hands with a raincoat sleeve, nudged the boots with her foot. Then made for the stairs. The raincoat kept guard over the empty hall.

The stairs were carpeted pale green. Spotless, with that brushed-up, recently hoovered look. Who on earth had time to hoover stairs? The elegant wooden banister gleamed, its struts immaculate, dust-free. Such cleanliness shouted loud as a trumpet. How much time did Catherine have to put in to achieve it? Vinny, by contrast, was a slut. A slattern. Sloppy and slovenly and slipshod. She rolled the consonants over her tongue and sang them under her breath.

On the tiny landing she hesitated. Three doors confronted her, all shut. Sturdy and panelled, painted glistening cream. Two on the right and one on the left. In the dividing space between them was a mahogany chest of drawers with curly edges and legs. The wood was polished to such a deep shine it hardly seemed wood any more. Just brown silk made solid. On top were some antique china dishes in blue and green with gilded scrolls for handles, a three-armed candlestick wreathed with gold leaves and roses. Three paintings of poppy-strewn cornfields hung on the walls.

The three doors bristled at her and shouted keep out. One of gold and one of silver and one of brass. A dragon or an aged hag or the handsome prince. You choose.

Vinny chose all three. First she opened the door in the middle. A rose-carpeted bathroom with a large window filmed in muslin, green plants on the low window-sill, a chintz-covered armchair. Next she tried the door on the left. A study with books all over the floor, a wooden Noah's Ark on a side table, a computer on a desk, a sofa. The door on the right opened into a bedroom. The casement window, its curtains drawn back, was framed by sturdy stems of clematis starred with white flowers, and beyond it a blur of treetops, moving silently in the night wind. As a child she'd found that frightening: trees that waved to and fro outside shut glass and made no sound. She had been unable to stay alone in a room with that view. Too menacing. She'd had to shout for Catherine to come and rescue her. Her hands longed to close the curtains, blot out the dancing trees.

As she hovered, something else crashed into her consciousness. The scent of the flowers? A nosegay of blue anemones and hyacinths in a tall glass stood on the table beside the bed. The bed. She was standing next to it. She had crossed the room without noticing. No choice. The painting hung in here summoned your eyes urgently. You were pulled close to it. A big painting. A six-by-four canvas that dominated the room, seemed to take up all the space. A female nude. Seen from the side, arching back on a salmon-pink bedcover, knees up and parted, one arm flung wide; the other arm crossing the belly, hand reaching between the bent legs; head tipped back, half-turned to one side. You couldn't see the young model's features. Her hair was hidden inside a turban and her face was deliberately blurred, screwed-up in ecstasy. Her intensity leaped out at you like a shout or a punch. The brushwork was urgent and flowing as waves of body heat. The thickly stroked-on paint did not mimic the sensuality of flesh but was it. Solid. Rippling. Worked with such ferocity it made Vinny exclaim out loud.

What was it like to lie in bed and look at that picture? Presumably it was Robert's work. Was it a turn-on? Perhaps Adam and Catherine just looked at it dispassionately. Well-manipulated paint. Vinny needed some distance from it. She backed away and turned to inspect the rest of the room.

The walls were the same pale pink as downstairs. The carpet was white; tight lamby curls of wool. The bed was an ornate French confection with whorled ends. A white cover traced with an embroidery of blue and yellow flowers in twists of silk. Antique. A heap of ancient cushions, the satin cracked, in faded rose. Vinny sank down into plump softness billowing up around her, and looked at the picture again. There was something familiar about it. Like a back glimpsed across the concourse of a railway station. Gesture. Attitude. Now she knew exactly where she had seen that composition before.

Click. She swivelled her head and started. Adam was standing in the doorway.

– Sorry, he said: didn't mean to make you jump.

They glanced at each other, then quickly looked away. He walked across to where she sat on the bed. To Vinny, still slightly stoned, he seemed to do it in slow motion. He took twenty-seven years to reach her. He pushed away a separating block of air. A skyscraper of words never spoken. Now he was close enough to touch. There was an exquisite pleasure, corkscrewing inside her like pain, in not lifting her hand, not reaching out towards him. In behaving herself just as she ought. An electric current discharged itself across her shoulder-blades. She stared straight ahead in order not to look up at his face. His jeans were Levi's 501s. The blue corner of one front pocket was torn.

– It's quite something, isn't it? Adam said.

Vinny made her mouth work. Her lips felt lazy and huge. She lived behind them, mumbling and clumsy. Speaking was like stumbling out of a soft cave.

– I shouldn't have come up here without asking first, she said: I suddenly got overtaken with curiosity.

Adam sat down next to her on the bed. Her insides turned over. He smelt faintly of soap and cigarettes. A good smell. He smelt exactly as he always did, exactly the same as he used to, twenty-seven years ago.

– I'd never seen that picture before we came here, Adam said: Robert must have kept it under wraps all this time.

Pleasure pushed along Vinny's arms and legs. Flesh melted to liquid gold. She wanted to go out of control, take him in her arms, draw him down to lie with her on this soft bed. Hold each other and kiss for a long time, feel her bones start to tingle and ache, her cunt fatten and swell.

– Do you know when it was painted? she asked.

– Nineteen seventy-four, said Catherine's voice: it's signed and dated on the back.

She was standing in the doorway, a plump, black-haired man in a black leather jacket just behind her.

Adam and Vinny got up. The four of them stood in a row and looked at the painting.

PART FIVE

Oh my dear master,

I ache for you. You don't know and you don't care.

I dream of you touching me.

I first learned what I liked in childhood. All those years of sharing beds; of course we all learned. Evening classes: our secret congresses in the middle of the night, huddled under quilts; playing and telling stories; tickling and caressing each other. Sometimes we pushed the beds together, end to end, so that we could tunnel through the bedclothes towards each other. In winter it grew dark at four o'clock and we were sent upstairs at seven. Too early for sleep and so we romped, careful not to make a din and rouse Aunt or Tabby. Like a nestful of kittens clambering over each other, biting and licking and nuzzling. I dream about playing with you like that, Monsieur. The lovely smell of you and me coming. Because I've cried out I wake up, and it's dawn in the parsonage, Arthur fast asleep next to me, a bleak grey sulking at the window-sill below the curtain edge. I kneel there and write this letter by that glimmer of arriving day.

Shall I tell you one of the differences between us? You know how to satisfy your appetite but I cannot satisfy mine.

You eat dinner in the early evening with Madame Heger. Pupils tidied away into silent rows in the refectory, children packed off upstairs. Only on Sundays were your little ones allowed to disturb the sacred peace of your dining-room. A bowl of vegetable soup with a crusty white roll, a dish of stewed onions, perhaps a slice of cheese, a piece of fruit. You see I remember your taste for simplicity; I ate supper with you both often enough at the beginning. You eat as much as you want and no more. Later on you go up to bed with Madame Heger and you make love. Proof of that: your tribe of little children. How many have you got now: eight? nine?

All this is possible because you believe in yourself; you believe in your life, that your wife adores you, that you have a future. You believe in a succession of days like this one unrolling in front of you, and that makes you happy and contented. You are master of your own life. You believe that the future will bring you more of this fulfilment.

If I had confidence in tomorrow, that it will come; that food for my soul will come; a letter from you; if I were able to believe in a future; a future of desire gratified; then I would be able to be calm. Emily had her God, dear master; she lived on the life of the spirit and the pursuit of poetry; but I cannot. I go into the kitchen where Martha is doing the week's baking and break off pieces of pastry crust, lick the wooden spoon pushed round the bowl of cake mixture, wet my finger and press it to the tabletop to collect crumbs.

You threw me crumbs, Monsieur, in those days when you replied to my letters. Tiny leftover scraps from your plate that

I grovelled in front of as a Catholic kneels to receive Holy Communion. Then I fell upon them and they were gone. I gnawed at the half-eaten crusts on the floor under your table like a ravening dog. I fought other dogs for your leavings.

Then you stopped writing to me and forbade me to write to you.

I see no future. There is only this now, this starving imperative, this open demanding mouth silently calling your name. Yet I am supposed to have everything I need. A roof over my head, a loving husband, a devoted father, duties to keep me busy, three meals a day. How dare I say that I want more?

But. But. I also want you, dear master. *Vous me manquez.* You are lacking to me. I lack you. My real self is not here in Haworth but at your side. Living abroad; with you. My real self is not this vicar's wife, this good daughter, but that young pupil-teacher, that disciple, ardently in love with you. Writing essays and stories. Planning her novel. My real life stopped when you rejected me and got rid of me.

I had no mother. No mother I could know or remember. I was too young when she died. No images of her that I could keep, precious treasures, in my memory. I stoppered up my child-self; all its longings. Only in reading and writing could they emerge and live freely. Only when I met you and began to love you. Then out they leaped, and they are in the world now, roaming free, genies out of their bottle; they will never go back in; they are grown too large too fierce too wild.

I'm emptied and hollowed out by this not having; by this wanting. There is no comfort for me. Where should I find comfort in this desolate place where it rains every day and mist blots out the lane beyond the garden wall and no-one ever comes to visit us?

Last night I dreamed of you and also I dreamed I was a girl again. I climbed into Emily's bed and pushed myself into her arms, pressed against her thin body under the thick flannel nightdress. After a bit she threw me off saying I was too heavy. Her chest was a cave of thin ribs; round as a hazelnut; there was no rest there. Leaning on her I thought she might break. Like a chicken when you've stripped the carcass and all that's left is a bony shell with nothing inside. Emily, my dream-sister, cannot be a mother to me. She is too thin. She might crack and shatter under my weight. I bear her down but she cannot bear me up.

All these parts of myself I cannot show to you, dear master. You must not see them. Not legs and petticoats: I don't mean that. I mean my need, my desperation. My desire. That's much too heated and shameful to put on show. Swaddle my mouth therefore in shawls and scarves and the pages of prayerbooks.

To appear before you, to be allowed to exist in your presence, I must be clean and happy. Not baring my teeth but smiling neatly like the other girls in class reciting the rules of composition and grammar to their *cher professeur*.

But I'd like to steal into your house, Monsieur, steal you and steal off with you, tender morsel in my mouth; I'm the fox carrying off your chickens, you my chicken, my pet; I'll smash your eggs and suck them I'll suck you dry.

Save me from this urge towards destruction, dear master. Tell me off. Tell me to behave. Only allow me to come and see you. Write to me. Allow me to believe that you receive this letter and that one day soon you will reply to

your devoted

Charlotte

PART SIX

Catherine was trapped in mess. A trail of litter connected one room to another. Half-full glasses jostled in the hearth, on the edges of bookshelves. The butts of lipstick-smeared cigarettes had been tossed into the fireplace, stubbed out in the earth of pot plants, left to float, swollen and disintegrating, in wine dregs. The ashtrays were little hills of feathers, overflowing; drifts of grey flakes were caught in the creases of rucked-up rugs, or powdered across the floor. The crumbs of shattered potato crisps crunched underfoot. Stray peanuts lodged, greasy and chipped, between floorboard cracks. The air stank of stale nicotine. Plates, set down anywhere, on chair seats or on the sofa, were smeared with leftover food. Like the dirty haloes of disgraced angels; abandoned where they fell. Like dirty snow. The room was awash, as though it had recently contained a glacier, just melted with the overnight coming of spring; the ice covering was gone; it had swept out, leaving its murrain behind. Under that pure white crust was only a morass of filth.

Adam wandered in from the hall, clutching a glass of whisky.

– We should drink to Robert's show. Charlie really means it, you know. Dad would have been so pleased.

– You should drink to me as well, Catherine said: I'm the one who took him up to see the picture.

Adam tipped back the last of his whisky. It got him to sleep better than the sleeping-pills the doctor had prescribed. Pills made you wake up feeling groggy, as though you'd been hit over the head; heavy and dry-mouthed. Whisky attacked more subtly, a golden warmth in belly and heart spreading along your veins to weaken your knees, collapse you gracefully into oblivion.

– Charlie's thinking of rescheduling everything, Adam said: opening with Robert's show. Did I tell you?

– Yes, Catherine said: you did.

Ambling over to the fireplace and kicking a half-burned log, sending up a fan of red sparks, he irritated her by adding to the disorder. She needed nothing in the room to move. She would still it with her hands if necessary, as you kill a chicken by wringing its neck. Her fists were clenched against her sides. Now he was peering at the toppled stack of CDs. Oh God, don't let him put any music on. That would be too much.

She forced a calm smile on to her face.

– You go to bed. You know I like to clear up straight away after a party. Just leave me to get on with it.

Adam was drunk, but he stacked a tray with a wobble of empty bottles, plates and dishes, and wove with it into the kitchen. She followed with a tray of glasses.

– You're tired out, she insisted: it won't take me long and I promise I don't mind a bit.

He kissed her. His breath smelt of wine and whisky mixed. His cheeks were already stubbly, grazing hers. He stumbled out, and she heard him beginning to climb the stairs.

– Don't worry if you hear any strange noises, she shouted after him: it'll only be me.

Sometimes at night now, Adam woke her up, jabbing her with his elbow. Quick. There it is again. D'you hear it? Catherine listened, straining her ears into the darkness. Nothing. You imagined it.

Adam insisted the noise was Robert tramping to and fro downstairs. His characteristic tread; heavy-footed and determined. By day, if he was in the kitchen or the sitting-room, alone in the house, he heard Robert pacing to and fro overhead. Last week he had seen Robert in the back garden, dressed in his paint-spattered working clothes, peering in through the window. He mouthed through the glass that he'd come back for something he'd forgotten. After that Adam had begun keeping the curtains closed. You should believe me, he said to Catherine. Catherine had spread her hands wide, tilted them downwards, and looked at the empty air pouring off them. She repeated: you imagined it.

Catherine opened the windows, front and back, to let out the nicotine reek. A yellow smell, the colour of Caporal cigarettes in their maize paper. Sweet, damp air blew in from the black garden. She emptied ashtrays, ran round with a broom, shook the rugs out of the back door and replaced them. The dishwasher refused to function, so she washed up by hand. Soon ranks of up-ended glasses shone wetly on the rack, and in rows on a tea-cloth on the kitchen table, winking with soap bubbles from having been too hastily rinsed. She kept remembering the look on Vinny's face earlier that night, as she sat on the bed with Adam and tried, too obviously, not to gaze at him. With a damp rag she wiped Vinny away. She swept her into a plastic bag, which she knotted tight at the neck and chucked in the dustbin. She scoured her off the sink and rinsed her down the drain. With licked finger and thumb she briskly snuffed her out. She drowned her in bleach in the lavatory bowl of the downstairs cloakroom then flushed her away.

She took a shower then crept into bed. She fitted herself along Adam's long body, zigzag, her knees behind his, her arm curved over him, and felt his warmth. One day soon, perhaps, he'd start wanting sex again. She was supposed to wait patiently until that happened. She kissed the back of his neck. He grunted in his pit of sleep. She began writing a new chapter in her head. That black leather chair at the hairdresser's. She would definitely do something with that. And a whip to tickle her heroine between her legs.

Catherine. Catherine.

A summons. Her name shouted out. The teacher at primary school taking the register, counting her into class? No, it's a lawyer. The prosecuting counsel. His voice is high and light. He reads aloud from a document, labels her the accused. She's in court.

86

She jerks upright in bed. Night, black as printer's ink. She's a character in a thriller. Someone's writing her in, pinning her down on to the page. The words unreel in the darkness, clear as subtitles on a cinema screen. The clock marks the seconds of anxiety. Bang on four a.m. She's been woken by a bolt of heat; like being struck by lightning. She mops her brow and cheeks with a corner of the sheet.

Her voice comes out as no more than a squeak. Not guilty.

Catherine wants to disappear. Thick with humidity. Made of nothing but this hot flesh, this sweat crawling over her skin like grease. She flaps the sheet under her chin, trying to trap a current of cool air. Make the memories melt off her and flow away.

She reaches for the glass of water on the table by the bed. Careful not to bump or chink, not to wake Adam who sleeps on by her side as though nothing is happening. But the bedroom is re-forming itself, rising around her in tiers of mahogany, she cowering at the bottom of the pit gazing up at the judge, and beside him and above him boxes of witnesses pointing their fingers and denouncing her. The heat is stifling. Water rises and rinses her brow, flows down the sides of her face. Flapping black gowns and curled horsehair wigs and red-faced men.

Now her nose was running. She turned on her side and groped under her pillow for a handkerchief. Nothing there. She got up, felt her way to the door. In the bathroom she blew her nose on a tissue, opened the bottle of Adam's sleeping-pills and swallowed one. Then she crept back into the bedroom, closing the door behind her with a tiny click, inching across the carpet so as to make no sound. She rolled into bed and drew the covers around herself.

She was shivering. Adam, turned away from her, was a dark mound, face in the pillow. Snoring gently. The rasp of this breathing, like a rusty clockwork engine being wound, was a comfort. She wanted to press her face between his shoulder-blades, but feared the caress would waken him. Instead she listened to his night-time purr and laid one hand lightly against his spine.

She tried to distract herself from anxiety by going over her planning for tomorrow. Finish clearing up. Go out, to leave Adam in peace for writing. Find dishwasher warranty and place by phone. Finish writing notes for next week's teaching. Email the boys. Do the ironing. Make a start on the new chapter of the novella. Decide whether or not to get rid of Robert's tapes completely.

When he was on his own, in between visitors, in the hospice, he'd talked into a tape machine. Some kind of memoir, she supposed. He'd given her the tapes to take away. They're a secret, mind. Don't tell Adam. Not till you've typed it all out. This is just between you and me, sweetie. I want it to be a surprise. Promise? Unwillingly, she'd promised. She'd slung the unlabelled tapes into a shoebox and pushed it to the back of the wardrobe, where it could be forgotten, lost. Old man, old man, don't hassle me. But perhaps she'd bury the tapes in the dustbin along with all the party rubbish. Without listening to them. Adam would never know.

Sleep grabbed her like a jailer, frogmarching her back into the tribunal, slamming her into the dock. The voice plucked at her with impatient hands. The voice belonged to Vinny. Whether or not Catherine told herself she was wide awake; she was fretting and therefore imagining things; Vinny's voice would not go away.

She was addressing her as though she were continuing a conversation they had begun a long time ago. They'd been interrupted and now they had resumed. It was like being tuned into a radio station and forbidden, by some unseen power, to switch off.

If Catherine was in the dock, Vinny was a witness for the prosecution. She was determined to speak. She wanted to put her side of the story.

Part Three

PART SEVEN

When we were children, *cher* Monsieur, Emily and I shared a room. Our beds were side by side. Summer nights, up here under the roof, were hot and airless. A dormer window above Emily's bed meant she could see the stars when she knelt up in her welter of blankets and coverlet. She liked to keep the window open; to feel the air on her face as she was falling asleep. If we forgot to wedge the wood-framed square of mesh in place then moths whirred in. Moonlight poured through that porthole, our floor scoured to silver like a scrubbed deck, and then the white flood setting our beds afloat, rocking and bumping and we in them turning to fish. The cotton curtains, drawn back, framed the moon, a white fruit on a black plate. I used to want to eat the moon. It hung above me, one of those cherries you called *coeur de pigeon.* We ate them for breakfast in June, do you remember, when we went out from Brussels to the countryside and breakfasted at a farm. Milk, rolls and butter, new-laid eggs, cherries. You fed us well, Monsieur. You liked to see us eat. Emily sat on the grass, tipping up her earthenware cup, and you watched her, smiling. She was healthy then. She was thin and brown and full of energy.

When I was little I was not clear that she was she and I was I. Night after night I tested her to find out where she ended and I began. In the darkness I could not see my sister but I knew that she was there. Whether or not I'd seen her undress or get into bed didn't matter. The blackness of night took us into itself and altered our forms, changed us into quite other creatures. She might have become a bat and flapped back out of the window, or a mouse, skulking back down its hole. On nights that she remained herself, Emily, and I Charlotte, I waited until I could bear our separation no more. Five minutes. Two minutes. I heard her breathing, or the rustle as she turned over inside the coil of blankets and sheets. Let me in with you, I'd whisper, then slide out of my bed, bound across the strip of cold oilcloth that formed the strait between us, turn back her covers, and slip into her warmth.

How different her bed felt from mine. Because she was in it, I suppose, taller than I was, so her indentation in the mattress a different shape. I learned her body by pressing mine into the mould she made with hers. We shared this hollowed-out place; we both fitted into it, like two almonds inside the same casing of nut, one concave and one convex. We curved, one to the other. Sometimes we lay face to face, arms around each other, and whispered to one another, her breath mixed with mine, hands pressing shoulder-blades. Sometimes she turned me over and used me as a blackboard, writing on my skin with her fingertip, while I squirmed and giggled; words for me to guess.

My sister Emily taught me how to write and read. You

didn't need eyes for this. You didn't need candlelight. Hands on flesh her writing implements, and my reading an intake of breath, delight at the cool movement of her flitting touch. My wish for her to go on and not stop led to understanding longer sentences; it was that simple. She traced whole stories on my back; she spelled out poems, line by line, all down my spine. When she'd finished, she twisted around, and I began. It was my turn. I wrote for her the stories of Angria. I acted them out with my hands smoothing her back, her waist. My sister: my first reader; my first audience; as I hers. Both of us writers and both of us readers, connected by the need for storytelling not to end. What happened next? And so then? Go on, go on.

That was how the bed-plays began. Bed-plays means playing in bed, and it also means writings made in bed. Dramatic writings. Her bed for stage; our sheets for backdrop and curtains. Battles and insurrections and love-making and cutting off the heads of enemies, one by one. All achieved in the dark by two small girls. Lover means writer and reader, yes)that's what it means, *mon cher* Monsieur.

But I lost my lover and so I married Arthur Nicholls. What hope was left to me? You were gone. My sister too. Both of you plucked away from me. We would never be together again. What was I to do in my loneliness? I wanted a companion. There was no-one. The silence was shrivelling me up like wisps of charred paper in the ashes of yesterday's fire.

Sometimes, at night, I dreamed of Emily wheeling through the cold stars, turning and turning among them as though she were now indeed one of them, as in life she always longed to be. When I woke up I would weep. She was lost to me for ever. On such nights the universe was brilliant as ice, and Emily utterly distant because she belonged to it in ways I did not. She was rock and tree and snow and torrent and heather whereas I crept about, clothed in a brown frock and brown boots and hat, to sit in church stuttering psalms to wheezy organ music. Emily was buried in church, under a stone slab. But she was not there. How could she possibly be there? She belonged outside, as she had always done. Once she was warm, and felt the sun on her flesh, and when I cried in bed at night, for some childish distress, for some harsh reprimand I felt I had not deserved, she would put her arms around me and say now Char, now Char. Now she is one with the rushing wind and the stream and the boulders that line the stream. I do believe that. I want to believe it. She is there.

One cold spring day, I remember, I'd been out, visiting a sick parishioner on a distant farm. I was walking home along the ridge of the moor. Suddenly I felt her with me. She was there in the wind over the stubby grass, the wind-blunted thorn trees leaning away from the white dust of the track. She was the wind and the birds calling each other and the bright line of water like a silver crack on the moor.

Sometimes she appears to me in human shape, when she is

no less removed from me. When I wake up I know it was only a dream, that I'm supposed to push it aside, as unimportant. Nothing to do with the business of the bright day. Yet while I'm in it the dream is the most real thing, and Emily too. Dreams are more true than daytime; in them I go down to a new country, one that I recognise is most surely my home, where I find all those who have vanished and left me; all those I love.

Even in daytime, sometimes, I'll suddenly find myself there.

It begins with a queer physical feeling that creeps up on me. The skin on the top of my head starts to tighten and pucker up, closing like the fontanelle of a baby that's just been born. The skin between my shoulder-blades similarly twitches and draws together, as though it has been loose and is now being tightened like strings. All my flesh is alive, dancing, as though stung with invisible pinpricks. My insides begin to turn over and over; I'm falling downhill; and I want to cry; and I want to make love; and my arms fly open searching for what's not there. I dissolve, yet I'm also utterly present, tingling all over with life coursing through me; all these changes in me and in the atmosphere signal that something is up; there is some disturbance; don't be afraid; but something or somebody is here even though you cannot see them; and all the time that fizzing feeling creeps about my back. Yes, like when I was a child lying in bed with Emily and she stroked me and whispered her truths. I want to cry and to come and I open my eyes and I see her.

Ghost is not the right word. Or, at least, if it is not adequate, I should have to say why. Ghost is the word people use after a vision, to put it away at one remove from themselves, to deny the validity of their perception, that the experience described did happen. If I say I believe in ghosts you can shrug and smile and suggest I am superstitious and foolish. So I shan't say I believe in ghosts so much as I believe in Emily. Incarnate, here, now, in some way I don't understand. She's not a remnant or a revenant, not an image of someone who's absent, not the shadow of herself, not pale or see-through or otherwise unworldly. Yes: she comes to me now from somewhere else, but she is here; she is real; she is my sister; she has never left me; I know her and I could not possibly feel afraid when she comes. There is only joy.

There is some humour, too, in these visitations. She puts on an appearance that will help me recognise her, in her changed being. She invokes those folk tales that used to enchant us when we were little. She's not afraid of borrowing items of angels' costume, of announcing herself with touches of gothic atmosphere. I think she does it to make me laugh. That's another way to know it's Emily – her silly jokes. Once she came to me on a shaft of sound, of music that was light, forming a silvery tightrope: her passage into this world. She arrived in the house. I heard a high, unearthly voice singing upstairs, and went to see what was the matter. I was pulled towards the source of the music, the light, by the quality of the singing. It was a haunting voice; a haunted voice. I sped up the stairs as though my slippers had wings, and found

Emily in my bedroom. She was in her old white nightdress, barefoot, her hair undone flowing down her back. She was radiant and young, fifteen again. She was whole and unblemished and perfect and undamaged and she had come back from the dead to show me that.

Right at the end she was a little sack of bones huddled on the sofa, curled up on her side, her head lolling, her two enormous eyes like holes burnt in paper. Her coughs rattled her fleshless frame. In between coughs Emily whispered how black I looked, seated against the light. I can't see your face any more, Char.

After her death she returned to show me her face, in case I'd forgotten it. Alive with intelligence and humour. That smile that split her face; a child's grin.

She came to cheer me up, to tell me that she was all right now, that I was no longer to worry about her, that I should not hold on to my grieving as though to her body. I was to give up my sister and give up my weight of sorrow and return to the land of the living. I was to find another reason for going on. Grief was over and done with and buried and changed into this Emily who hovered in the sunlight in my bedroom and smiled at me.

I obeyed her. I woke up alone and bereft but determined to do whatever had to be done next. That turned out to be marriage to Mr Nicholls.

PART EIGHT

Grow up! Catherine yells at Vinny all through their adolescence. But Vinny clings on to certain childish habits. Even aged twenty-four she still doodles on pavements.

You buy chalk in tens or twenties, like cigarettes, rootling for the blue and white cardboard packets on the stationery shelf in the newsagent's. A fresh stick of chalk is smooth and cool, rolling between your fingers while you decide what to write. Soon your hands are smeary with white dust. Your sweat puts greasemarks on the chalk's clean skin.

Vinny buys coloured chalks too. Wiping her palms absent-mindedly on her face she gives herself green cheeks, a blue moustache, as though she's been to a clown workshop at a children's festival. Only afterwards, in the ladies' at the pub, does the mirror over the washbasin show her what she's done.

She keeps the chalks in her pocket, along with her keys, cash, handkerchief, notebook and pen, lip-salve. Women's clothes don't have proper pockets so she wears a man's jacket; double-breasted; worn striped lining and plentiful inner pouches with turned and stitched lips. When she bought the jacket in Brick Lane she slid her hands into these neat pockets, fiddled into their corners, digging around to check for relics. She found ridges of woolly dust, a mother-of-pearl button, a threepenny bit. The jacket skims round her. Laden with her bits and pieces, it doesn't bulge. It's like taking your own cupboard out with you. You can pack it with paperback books and your lunchtime sandwiches and nothing shows.

Vinny dons this roomy coat for her writing expeditions. She maps the city by treading across its pavements and writing on them where appropriate. In London the pavements seem grey until you study them, when you distinguish pale pink and pale green and cream. Pressure of weather and use makes them crack and tilt up, collecting rain. In the wet nights they shine, black reflectors, shimmer with oil rainbows.

Sometimes workmen prise up the broken paving-slabs from their bed of sandy grit, hammer new ones flat into place. Sometimes they peel them back, underworld lids, revealing coils of bright electric stems that sprout forth like jack-in-the-boxes, tangling bouquets of red yellow blue green flowers. You'll see the stooped back of a man sitting, patient and serious, indigo legs dangling, on the edge of a black pit, twiddling all the plastic wires like macramé. Knitting the city's secret veins and arteries back together again.

Fallen gravestones on other days the pavements seem to her, pressing down on the too lively dead to keep them in their place and stop them haunting passers-by in daylight. Underground, the coffins shunt about, breaking free from cemeteries, shooting the rapids of sewers, and their passengers only too keen to burst up in Nunhead or Kensal Rise for a taste of sunlight and the bitterness of traffic fumes on their rotted tongues.

Sometimes, though, pavements are just blank surfaces for writing on, like sheets of paper or schoolroom slates.

Outside certain houses in certain streets Vinny stops, stoops, and scrawls. A quotation, or the whole of a short poem; a name plus dates. The houses of famous writers are marked with blue plaques. So her services are not needed by Rimbaud and Verlaine in Mornington Crescent, by Mallarmé in South Kensington, by Doctor Johnson and Dickens in the City, by Defoe and Mary Wollstonecraft in Stoke Newington. She walks to these sites anyway. To pay her respects. Then progresses on her solo pilgrimage to other, unmarked shrines. Outside Jean Rhys's temporary rented room in Elgin Crescent she chalks her testimony. She pursues Katherine Mansfield and Dorothy Richardson and Dorothy Sayers down shabby-genteel streets in Kensington and Pimlico. She paces Cornhill seeking traces of Charlotte Brontë arriving to confront her unsuspecting publishers who think she's a man. She searches for the Chapter Coffeehouse where Charlotte slept.

Passers-by assume she is a hawker or a gypsy, leaving esoteric messages for her companions working parallel streets. They skirt her boot soles, splayed left hand, hunched dark back, and hulk past with their shopping bags and pulled toddlers. They can see she's not one of those pavement artists able to reproduce the Mona Lisa or the Last Supper in pastels. Is she a vagrant? Mentally retarded? A madwoman? Dogs sniff at her then wander on. She writes in the flowing and legible script she learned at primary school. After a shower of rain her words will wash away.

Dead people are Vinny's companions. They line the bright world with necessary shadow; silvery grey. In their subtle way they remain part of the living, roving the streets as she does, packing into buses, jostling in the corners of shops. The dead love the living and don't want to be parted from them. Or perhaps it's envy, that we still have blood in our veins and can kiss each other. Look, murmur the dead: soon you're going to end up like me. The land of the dead presses in on us from all sides. That was how the Anglo-Saxon writer saw it, too: life the brightness, noise and jollity of the great hall that the sparrow darts through so briefly; death the enormous surrounding darkness, the mystery from which the sparrow came and to which it must return.

Each of us walks with a crowd of the dead at our backs, tugging them along like bunches of invisible balloons. Vinny welcomes their approach. She wants to be connected with them. She searches for them. They often congregate in derelict places where they can set up camp and not be disturbed. Boarded-up yards behind abandoned factories, Victorian school playgrounds awaiting conversion into the patios of luxury flats: in these pockets of older use tucked into the modern townscape the city swarms with ghosts.

They fly in the sunlight like specks of dust. Layers of them hover in the air she breathes just outside garden gates. The hands of the dead carted scuttles of coal four flights of stairs up from that cellar whose silvery lid shines just in front of the porch. Smoothed up that wallpaper palimpsest. Dusted that gas-mantel. Set jellies in that larder.

Dead writers are her way into the community of the dead in general. Dead writers, if she can track down the pavements over which they once trod, the beds in which they slept and made love, clarify and redefine her city, help her find her place among the living. By discovering their haunts she becomes an agent. She acts. The city becomes manageable, begins to make sense. She plants her own signposts around it, stringing together its parts into her own patterns. Everyone does that. Her parents did, while they were alive; before they died of cancer. First one, and then the other. Father. Then mother. Vinny was twenty-one, Catherine twenty-two when their mother died. Babes in the wood. Her parents had tried to scatter trails of white breadcrumbs through the urban forest for them to follow. But then they got lost and birds flew down and ate the crumbs. The sisters went on, hand in hand; got on with life. Nothing else to be done.

Vinny doesn't inscribe the kerbs outside the houses of living writers. Phantoms they may be for readers who never meet them, but nonetheless it's mainly the unseen presences of the dead that fascinate. Written language, stored in books, let you travel backwards, through and beyond death. It let you stand in the presence of the person who made it. Perhaps five hundred years before.

At secondary school, still in Catherine's footsteps, she

learned that great literature lasted for ever, because of the eternal verities it enshrined about the human condition, and thus conferred immortality on the writer. The book, in this version, became a substitute for the body. Great writers died and their bodies decayed but their books lived for ever.

Vinny didn't see it that way. She saw simply the words. This poem was made in the seventeenth century. The structure of its grammar, twist of metaphors, spelling, cannot be faked up by a later time. It is utterly authentic. It is itself. In its presence I am therefore also in the presence of its making. When I read it I am living in the seventeenth century, witnessing its formation. Reading is a form of time travel. Reading is a form of resurrection, a past time resurrected as the reading of the poem is made. There is no death in this sense. No death of language. Language goes on, despite death, the skein that binds the generations, making itself new between the life and death of every poet. Language is as certain as death but triumphs over it.

So you didn't need religion. What you needed was poetry. Immortality was embodied inside language itself, did not exist separately from it.

This could only happen with poetry she considered good. Bad poems' language might have weathered down over a couple of centuries to become intriguing or quaint, but the poem remained a fossil, merely an image of something once alive. Most criticism was fossil-like, too. Only the very best survived like a good poem. Because – why? Because the language of criticism depended on theories that wore out as they became unfashionable and were replaced. Whereas the language of poetry and novels was hammered out of something else; metaphor; purer and sparer. Like bones and blood. Clothes changed from generation to generation, but flesh was flesh. And poems were like bodies. Bodies with souls. Language was the soul? Poetry was the soul? That part of us which went on and did not die. So heaven was literature.

When she wasn't working at her part-time research job for a children's charity Vinny prowled London. She inscribed the London pavements as a way of paying homage to writers London had sheltered, writers she admired and whom she considered undervalued. Fetishistic perhaps but she didn't care. She wanted to draw attention to these inspiring writers. Other people wrote newspaper articles on such subjects. She recorded the writers who wrote beautiful books and flitted, poverty-stricken, debt-ridden, escapees from lovers or land-ladies, from one cheap let to another. She pointed to them with chalk arrows. With chalk nails she banged up melting and dissipating plaques.

When she told Catherine she wanted to do this outside Adam's house, that he was a living writer aged twenty-six whom she had actually met, her sister remarked: sounds like you're joining the real world at last.

Vinny encountered Adam first of all in a bookshop.

She flagged the meeting in her diary. Four o'clock on 30 November 1973. The eve of All Souls. Vinny Delamare, aged twenty-four, entered Colet's bookshop in the Charing Cross Road. For the purpose of browsing. She wanted something to read over a cup of coffee in Maison Bertaud while she waited for Catherine, whose teaching job often kept her late.

She saw herself in the shop assistant's assessing gaze. She was wearing blue platforms with puckered elasticated ankle straps, a skimpy cheesecloth smock, flared embroidered loons with buttoned fly, a man's dinner jacket. Short hair, one diamanté stud earring and one pearl, no makeup. Face and hands powdered with white chalk. Was she a bit of street theatre? Her coat obviously had large pockets. She could be a shop-lifter, so at first the assistant kept an eye on her, then lost interest, and swivelled back to her till.

Vinny's method was to approach the table of new publications, close her eyes, pick at random.

She opened her eyes. Looked down at her hand. *The Angel in the Cupboard*. A novel by Adam Shepherd. The book was a pleasure to hold and opened easily. Thick laid paper, cream-coloured. Roman typeface, twelve-point. She dived in. Standing by the table in the centre of the shop, leaning on it with one hand, holding the book up in front of her with the other. Then, as it drew her into itself, she walked away into one of the alcoves between the stands of bookshelves and propped her shoulders against the wall.

The world tilted she lurched missed her footing almost fell. A great silence everything was stilled she held her breath outside changed place with inside. With one part of her mind she knew she was standing in a cold damp bookshop in Charing Cross Road, the ribbed gas fire sputtering yellow and blue, two other customers braying haw-haw at each other, but none of that mattered, and her surroundings now began to recede because in front of her were these words curved and black like a wrought-iron screen and now she had slipped through and was inside.

First the world cracked open and tossed itself up into the air in bits, then recomposed itself fell back into shape after that great breaking and put itself back together on the page as this sentence. Everything every single word was now in its right place; she could feel that in her own flesh, the rightness of it; she could see how the world and her body were one, held so lightly, breathed into being; how fragile and yet how solid; she could see each word and their connections, the whole and the parts. It was a huge consolation: the world was mended and she herself too; everything had been reshaped and she along with it; everything was in order again; a new order; this was beauty, this pattern never seen before, shining and perfect; it lived and breathed and was whole; it was so right she wanted to fall down to cry and laugh to explode.

She was yawning and the shop was closing and so she had to come out of her dazed and blissful state because the assistant was turning out the fire and the lights and shooing out the customers with irritated cries. All of them, not just Vinny, lurched out into the street like lovers reluctant to part. No paper bag for her book. She clutched it in her ungloved hands, along with the flyer advertising Adam's forthcoming reading, and went to Maison Bertaud. She ordered a cup of coffee. Opened the book again.

Catherine was practical when she arrived, untwirling her

III

long stripy scarf and throwing her Greek shoulder-bag on to the floor under the Formica-topped table.

– Go to the reading. It's obvious. I'll come with you if you like.

– No thanks. I'll go on my own.

In this photograph Vinny looks younger than twenty-four. Big eyes, wide mouth, cropped hair sticking up in tufts. Flawless skin. Lips pinched shut and forbidden to smile. She's trying to seem cool but failing. That intense, wavering look of someone who's stoned. She wears a sleeveless sequined waistcoat over flared blue jeans and her blue platform heels. Brown slender arms. Roll-up balanced between her fingers. No, it must be a joint. She leans back on a purple floor cushion, which is propped against the side of a low double bed. Pelvis tilted at the ceiling, long legs crooked up splayed out open in front of her, displaying her neat denim crotch.

She's been up half the night since the gig ended. Last week they watched a performance artist bury himself alive in a tiny dugout under an art gallery in Marylebone; this week they applauded, when he'd tunnelled out under the road and erupted on the other side like a large mole. She came back to Adam's flat in Bethnal Green. He's the first person she's met, of her peers, to have a place of his own; even though it's rented. They've been playing with the camera, listening to music, passing books of poems back and forth and reading bits out to each other. She's warm and floaty from pints of beer in the pub and then red wine back here in Adam's room, and now spiralling higher, smoking dope.

She wants him so much it's hard to speak, let alone sound remotely intelligent. She can't get the words on to her tongue; too swollen and thick; and when she does blurt something out she exaggerates and sounds stupid. She chooses poems to read out that are clever and funny. Nothing to do with desire, with love, with sex. Trying not to give herself away.

She can't talk truly because she can't touch. If she could only touch him that would convey everything she wants to say. Touch is subtle talk better than words. No, that's not true; it's just that she wants to touch him as well as talk with him; her words would come right if she could only touch him at the same time. Her fingers ache with the effort not to reach out.

She hauls herself upright, from where she's slipped down the cushion, and frowns at her feet. Bad girl don't touch bad girl. This is the mad logic of her Catholic girlhood: what you want must be forbidden so because it's forbidden you want it you can never have it bad girl. Round and round you go forgetting you can have and you can want and you can not have and you might get. She wants to peel his clothes off and kiss him top to toe. At home they had a kitten once, which used to perch on Vinny's shoulder and lick her face and neck with its little rasping tongue; she'd like to do that to Adam, lick him all over, and she'd like him to do it to her too, and she'd like to hold his penis, stroke it between her hands, kiss it, lick it. Catholic girls weren't supposed to want to do that either. You had to tell the priest about it on Saturday night. Unchaste thoughts. It was better not to have them so you didn't have to mention them to the priest.

Saturday night. Three in the morning. Vinny and Adam have known each other for two weeks. A long time, in terms of their world, in terms of fancying someone and telling them so. It was simple to meet him. She went to his reading, approached him afterwards, told him how much she liked his novel. She hung around, became part of the group that went to the pub. She has been for walks in the park with him, has gone drinking with him, has shared a curry with him after a gig. They have discovered they have both lost their mothers. Adam's ran away. That's as much as he will say. Now he sits a foot away from her, flicking over the pages of the book, looking so self-contained she's in despair.

She must have got it all wrong. Perhaps he's in a panic, regretting he ever invited her back. Probably he doesn't fancy her at all. He really only cares about literature. She doesn't feel able to say any of this. What's the protocol anyway? No rules these days about who makes the first move. Women's liberation lets you claim your desire, but nonetheless men don't always like it, and you don't want to be insensitive, trying to get off with someone who's not interested. Actually, liar, yes, you do. You'd like to be able to interest him. Seduce him with amazing subtle feminine power so that he's hardly aware of what's happening but still he's yielding, he's doing exactly what you want, pulling you into his arms, stroking your breasts. Vinny doesn't know how to tiptoe up to him and render him putty in her hands. She wishes she were the sort of woman you meet in novels, who just radiates a soft feminine sexuality that has the hero madly in love with her within three seconds. She's terrified of sounding like a sergeant major barking orders. Trousers off! Into bed!

Adam goes on reading.

She tells herself not to be in such a rush. Enjoy the moment. Take your time. Why be in such a hurry?

She watches her hand bound across the space of amber rug between them and land, light as a grasshopper, at the edge of his thigh.

Apparently casual. Almost a mistake. So he doesn't have to notice. He can just go on reading to her, if he wants; he can pretend he doesn't know she's sent him a tiny message in sign-writing.

He halts. Looks up. Their eyes meet. She watches him read what her eyes convey and in the same instant reads what his eyes send back.

Both of them bump six inches towards each other along the rug.

Adam took that photograph. To Vinny, staring back at him holding the camera, it meant she was now properly in the room, part of it, not just looking on. Entering, she was still a voyeur. He tossed out the invitation above the hubbub in the pub. You can come back to my place if you like. OK, she answered. She was saying yes to sex. She assumed. That was the code. Going to a man's room meant sex. Once you were through his door you'd said yes. If you said no while you were in there it meant you were a cockteaser. Women's liberation hadn't yet changed that, though it might. Early days. She didn't know if he was sleeping with anyone else. She wouldn't have dreamed of asking. That would be possessive. That was the code too. Not being jealous of a man or making demands on him or assuming anything. Once that rubbish was cleared away you could make love freely. So men said. You tried to live up to their ideal. Sometimes you exploded with rage.

They wove along the street crowded with people bubbling out of the pubs, not talking much. Not touching. Vinny was suddenly so shy she couldn't think of anything to say.

Entering his bedroom in the shabby flat, she took a good swerving glance round. Before he turned off the lights and they hunched near the flame of the thick churchy candle stuck on a low iron spike. He had painted the walls a strong yellow, with a wide dark red stripe at waist level, dark red cornice and skirting-boards. She picked her way across the sanded floor between stalagmites of books, tossed-down clothes, sprays of folders and papers, a tray of used crockery, a heap of unmatched boots and shoes, a bright slither of albums circling the record player. The Band on top. He picked up the glossy square of cardboard, slid the record out, wiping the vinyl on his woollen sleeve, put it on the turntable. While he hovered over the needle, making sure it slotted neatly down, Vinny's glance swept over the low bed, a base propped on planks, half draped with an Indian spread in yellow and red Paisley, the desk in the corner, piled with more books and papers, the Grateful Dead and Che Guevara posters on the walls, the weeping fig and cheeseplant by the window-sill.

The gas fire bloomed into life. They parked themselves a foot apart on the dark yellow rug, sprawled against the edge of the bed, propped by floor cushions covered in purple velvet. Adam hooked his stash out from the wooden box he used as a bedside table and turned off the overhead light. He lit the fat white candles. Vinny took the tobacco tin from him.

– Let me.

She wanted him to see how well she could roll a joint. A modest three-paper one, the skins swiftly licked along their gummed edge then pressed into a single oblong sheet, chocolate curls of tobacco, fresh and damp, laid along it then fidgeted into the pinched crease, the lump of dope heated at one end with a lit match, smouldering fragrance, then this brown softness crumbled along the length of the tobacco bed, the whole thing twirled up between fingers and thumbs into a cylinder fattish at one end, rolled-up piece of cardboard slid in for a roach, twisted end lit. She inhaled the dark sweetness of the hit, passed the joint to Adam.

In the morning he crouched, naked and shivering, in front of the fire, lighting it, then pulled on an ancient frogged woollen dressing-gown and went off barefoot to forage for breakfast. Vinny liked the grey dressing-gown. She recognised another habitué of junk stalls and jumble sales. He reappeared with mugs of tea and a plateful of bacon sandwiches oozing butter, got back into bed with her. He put his arm around her and kissed her. The sheets were thin flannel, candy stripes now dingy and in need of a wash. Smelling of Adam's sweat. Vinny didn't mind the grubby sheets. It was how people were. Anyway, she liked Adam's smell. And now she had added her own smell to the mix.

They went out together at noon. A couple of ghosts flew up and followed them. One was Mum and the other was Dad.

Vinny flicked through her guidebook, a green oblong one the size of some folded legal document. Paragraphs of descriptive text were headlined in red, accompanied by sketched illustrations and little maps, suggestions of routes. Pneumatic Michelin men gambolled in the margins.

The book expected the reader to be touring by car. Tourism was the modern word, which denoted groups in planes and coaches. Touring was old-fashioned and individual. It suggested ladies wearing white dustcoats and veils tied over their hats, men with waxed moustaches posing with one foot on the running-board of the stately motor, wicker picnic-baskets strapped on behind. All to do with class. Tourism was middle to lower, touring was middle to upper. But Vinny and Catherine were taking the boat-train.

– Do you really not mind me coming too? Catherine asked.

Vinny had originally planned to journey alone. Adam, already in France, would meet her at the other end. She would have a solo adventure, travelling towards him, a bag of turmoil and desire placed primly on her lap, held down like a squirming cat. Now, a change of plan. All because of that night in the pub.

Catherine's trip to Wales with friends had fallen through. The others had decided to go to Venice instead and she hadn't the money to accompany them. She sounded glum on the telephone. Vinny imagined her twiddling a strand of hair, her mouth turned down. July, and it's raining, and I'm going to be stuck in bloody London all summer. Vinny tapped her cigarette on the yellow Ricard ashtray. She had arranged to go for a drink with Adam, but she wanted to cheer her older sister up. That was their silent pact since their parents' deaths: to comfort each other. As though that were possible. As though kindness were a quilt you could draw up over your nose and huddle under. As though it were a new skin patching the gaping wound. Better to stay numb. Cauterise the gash, the trunk of the tree torn away from the branch, with food, cigarettes, drink, sex. Vinny felt guilty, too. She was about to embark on delight, going to stay with Adam at his father's house, whereas Catherine had been let down, robbed of the prospect of happiness. She must share her own happiness with her.

Having something to offer Catherine made her feel

powerful. She almost blurted it out immediately: why don't you come with us to France? But she caught herself. She must ask Adam first. And it was his father's house, not hers. She couldn't just turn up with an extra guest without permission. So she said merely: come to the pub with us. You haven't met Adam yet, I'm sure you'll like him.

Catherine had made sandwiches for the journey. Wrapped up greaseproof-paper packets of white bread, plump with egg mayonnaise, fringed with wispy cress, for Vinny, thinly spread with cottage cheese for herself. They ate their picnic on the cross-Channel boat, sitting on the empty promenade deck watching England recede into the mist, then tossed the crusts to the seagulls screaming in their wake. Milky and rippling, it spread out wide in the shape of a V.

– V for Vinny, V for Victory, Vinny said.

They were perched side by side on the chilly cream-painted edge of a lifebelt locker, the wind whipping their hair and slapping their cheeks, making their eyes water. Puddles glistened in the dents of the battered surface of their makeshift seat and on the deck underfoot. Some were oily, with caught rainbows idling in them like fish. Above them black fumes fled up in furry columns from the steamer's funnel. The sky was grey, and the cold air smelt of smoke and salt. It left a gritty taste in your mouth. Both sisters wore fur-fringed Afghan waistcoats, red and white Palestinian scarves wound round their necks. They still felt cold. In between mouthfuls of sandwich they tucked their hands under their armpits and shivered.

Catherine licked her fingers, which had white smears on them. She brushed a shower of crumbs off the knees of her jeans.

– Do you mind me coming? she repeated: really?

– No, of course not, Vinny said.

In between truth and a lie. Bit late to ask that now. You could have thought of that earlier.

Vinny and Catherine had walked through the rain to the Mother Redcap in Camden Town to meet Adam. Disdaining umbrellas; parka hoods up. Out of the black, wet street into warmth, yellow light, the smell of beer and cigarettes. The three of them sat at a small round table and drank pints and smoked, heads bent together. Conversation had to be pushed across under the din of the juke-box playing early Buddy Holly. A sheet of cigarette smoke the sail on their freight of words, tugging guarded politeness back and forth. Yes, my father's a painter. Yes, he takes students for painting classes in the summer, but he's got a five-week gap this year. So we're going out. Yes, the house is quite old. A hundred and fifty years old, perhaps. Vinny hunched, smoothing her cigarette packet, half empty, soft, jiggling her box of matches, opening and shutting it; jack-in-the-box, no, puppet booth with Mr Punch jumping up to bash his babies' black heads. She watched the other two size each other up from behind their beer glasses.

Half an hour later, in the chilly, stinking Ladies', Catherine glared at the single cold tap dribbling into the rust-stained sink.

— He seems okay, she said.

She was looking around for something on which to dry her wet hands. She wiped them on her long skirt.

Vinny shouldered through to the bar and got whisky chasers for their pints. Coming back to their corner she stepped carefully, swerving through the pack of shouting drinkers, hands raised protectively, fingers laced around the three glasses. She planted these on the scarred brown table-top. Light shone on Catherine's red-gold hair, her skin. Her mouth was looser now she'd been drinking, less wary; she was half smiling as she listened to Adam. Her eyes, directed side-ways, glanced up at Vinny. Adam's blue eyes were looking down as he spoke intently. Then he glanced up too. She smiled at them both as she reclaimed her bentwood chair.

She had certainly wanted to show Adam off. Look: isn't he lovely? You're not the only one who can have proper lovers, Cath. She had hidden that boast under pretending to be relaxed, casual. He and she didn't have to be on their own all the time, did they? Also, three as a number felt so close, such a pleasing shape, such fullness, able to hold so much love, so perfect. Two was easy, but three required delicacy, balance, care. Three was good, too, because it meant you weren't shut-ting the third person out.

Vinny saw soon enough what was going to happen. Adam was generous and kind. He had plenty, and he was always ready to share with others. Books or beer or sweaters. He would jump in and offer. So when Catherine casually men-tioned that her own holiday had fallen through, Adam immediately invited her to accompany them to France.

Vinny bent her head over her whisky. She placed her hands round her glass, thumbs and fingers touching. If she was rough the glass might break and shards would cut her and she would bleed.

He hadn't consulted her. He hadn't asked her first. So he was in charge of their plans, not he and Vinny together. Vinny was pierced in the stomach. To muffle the wound she gave the pain a name: jealousy; possessiveness. Bourgeois individualism. Pain you should not feel, because it ran counter to ideas of collective virtue, and so she concentrated extremely and willed it away. She snatched a cigarette and took a gulp of her whisky. The sharpness and burn inside could have a new name: booze. Anyway she loved Catherine yes she did.

Don't you think, Vinny?

Oh yeah, great idea.

After a week it became true some of the time. To say what she felt was no longer possible, too complicated, and then it was buried, forgotten, like a dead mouse under the floorboards. Sticking-plaster over her mouth stretched in a smile at Catherine. Coward. But the arrangements had all been made. Too late to alter anything. Her feelings jumped about, not untangled until she was on deck, sitting next to Catherine, thinking. I'm in love with Adam. Mustn't tell him. Men hate that. Anyway I don't believe in romantic love do I. A delusion. A snare. Bourgeois ideology. Put it away, then, in her pocket, a secret to take out and study next time she is on her own. Or chuck it away now, cast it off, over-board, into the sea. Let it be gobbled up by hungry fish.

Adam's father lived outside the village of Sainte-Madeleine in the *département* of the Sarthe. Vinny and Catherine were to take the train from Calais to Paris, cross Paris by metro, take another main-line train from Montparnasse, then change on to the branch line for Sainte-Madeleine.

Now they were nearly on the last leg of the journey. Both of them suddenly weary of negotiating queues, crowded spaces. Under the high glass roof of Montparnasse station they felt sweaty and hot in the stale air smelling of *frites*. The main concourse was webbed with travellers and holiday-makers tugging children, little dogs, and carts of suitcases behind them. Passengers, arrivals and lookers-on milled doggedly back and forth. Whichever way you went it was always against the flow and you bumped into people. Voices exclaimed, the loudspeaker boomed, a transistor radio piped up eddies of pop music, soulful Johnny Hallyday, Sylvie Vartan soppy-sweet. The hubbub rose up in waves, banged back and forth.

Vinny's blue duffel slumped, grounded, heavy as a bag of sand, bulky with sharp-cornered objects that stuck out and hit your shins. Catherine, meeting Vinny at Victoria, watch-ing her struggle to lift this soft rock on to her shoulder, had tested its weight and frowned.

– Books, I suppose. Don't tell me. The complete works of Charlotte Brontë. Surely Adam's father will have books in his house?

– Not necessarily the ones I want to read, Vinny said.

She kept Catherine company at the station bookstall, flicking through fashion magazines. Pale models in skinny shifts. Blank-faced waifs dangling long matchstick limbs, splayed knock-kneed like puppets, toes turned in, huge panda eyes circled with black eyeliner, fringed with black false lashes. Looking as though they'd been abandoned, like lost luggage. Baby dolls waiting for someone to turn up and collect them. They made Vinny uneasy: they seemed so fragile, so vulnerable. The dead were safer. They were so innocent now they were at peace. They could no longer be hurt, and they could not hurt anybody either.

– Can we go and look at Montparnasse cemetery? Vinny asked: the guidebook says it's just round the corner.

– No time, Catherine cried, checking her watch: our train's in five minutes.

Vinny's clumpy sack slowed her progress through the elbowing crowd. It dragged at her legs from behind, brought her down, like a rugby tackle. Catherine seized a handle and towed her along, almost tripping. Shouting at her to hurry. They made the train steps with a minute to spare, hauling themselves up the steep little tier of black iron lace into the corridor. Into the first carriage they reached. Empty. They teetered in a muddle of bags, breathless and panting, Vinny grinning in triumph, Catherine still tense-faced. The whistle shrilled. Shouts from outside. The train jerked forward. They jolted, almost fell over. Then together they heaved the bags up on to the overhead rack, sat down. The train tick-tacked away, out into the concrete suburbs. Now Catherine could relax. Her shoulders unclenched and she flopped against the shiny leatherette backrest.

– We've done it, Vinny said.

– Just, Catherine said.

Vinny began ferreting in her shoulder-bag. She brought out bottles of Orangina, a bottle-opener, a packet of cigarettes. Catherine twisted round, knelt up on the seat, looked at her reflection. She fished out her comb and smoothed her hair. Vinny served them a bottle of Orangina each, lit up a Gitane. The rough taste hit the back of her throat, scorched its way into her lungs.

The train rocked out into the countryside, striking southwest through cornfields. They swigged their sweet fizzy drinks, finished their cigarettes, yawned. Soon Catherine put her head on her arm and fell asleep.

Half dozing, Vinny slipped away from being twenty-five, dissolved backwards. Became a baby again, held on Mum's lap and jogged very gently up and down. How soothing this rhythm, and the clattering of wheels on rails, so regular that it lulled you into dreaminess, melted you into the landscape you were speeding through, the sun warm behind the window and the little serge curtain rough against your cheek.

Up and down, up and down, up and down. She wanted never to stop but to go on for ever, part of this flow of goodness and sweetness and bliss; she could have as much as she wanted; she was full of love and pleasure and sleep.

Someone shook her by the shoulder.

– Wake up. We're nearly there.

She struggled awake. Tears wanted to spill. Mum was dead. Green sleep-grit to be knuckled from under her eyelids, hands sticky with heat and sweat. Her hair felt dirty.

By the time they halted in Sainte-Madeleine Vinny had had enough of trains.

She saw Adam immediately, at the other side of the booking-hall. He was just coming in through the far door with an older man who must be his father. Tall and stocky, with curly fair hair and piercingly bright eyes. Dressed in blue denim jacket and trousers.

Adam saw them and turned. He was unsmiling, tense. He hesitated, said something to his father, then came towards them.

Robert had one arm around her waist and one around Catherine's. He was kissing them, swivelling his mouth from side to side to plant smackers on their cheeks. Vinny and Catherine twisted in his embrace, trying to dodge. Adam looked on. Then he came forward and reached for Vinny's bag.

– Hi, Vinny, he said.

– Hi, Adam, she replied.

Robert tightened his grip on Catherine, and she subsided. She smiled at him weakly and politely. She turned her head and sent Vinny a sardonic look.

– Come on, darlings, Robert said: car's just outside.

Robert's house was called Les Deux Saintes. The four of them lived together in it for five weeks. At first Vinny thought it was like being in a commune. Soon she saw that this comparison was false. In a commune everybody was supposedly equal, whatever hierarchies rippled underneath that flat surface; whoever dominated in secret while pretending not to. But Robert made no fake display of democracy: he was definitely king of his castle, the rest of them dirty rascals. So then she thought: it's like having a second go at a family.

A fairytale one. The setting was out of those stories she'd devoured in childhood: the isolated house half-way up the hill, not quite the poor woodcutter's shack, but certainly on the edge of the forest, and plain enough. No wicked stepmother to be seen: the last applicant for the post had apparently been chased off on to the train for Paris. But present were the two resourceful motherless girls, herself and Catherine, the prince in disguise, Adam, all appropriately dressed in colourful and becoming rags, and the giant who could obviously be a bit of an ogre, Robert. Or are Cath and I the ugly sisters? Probably.

Her host further conformed to the archetype by preferring to live in his own, separate world, with his own customs and rituals. He took no part in the French country life going on around him. He had deliberately chosen the house, he explained over dinner the first night, because it was four kilometres outside the village and sufficiently distant from the nearest neighbours, the Beauvins in the farm down the road, for them not to bother him. Peace and quiet for his work, no having to waste time on people with whom he had nothing in common. His painting was all that mattered.

– And your love affairs, Adam muttered.

Adam had produced a spinach lasagne, the layers of pasta thin and light, the béchamel sauce flavoured with pepper and nutmeg and bay. When Catherine complimented him on it, Robert laughed.

– Adam's lasagne, that's nothing, that's the only thing he can make. Wait till you taste my moussaka tomorrow.

Vinny wished she were sitting facing the fire, instead of having her back to it. Scorched on one side and chilled on the other. Firelight gave you something to concentrate on, like a friend's face. Adam, seated diagonally across from her, didn't speak to her or catch her eye. He seemed diminished, thin, next to his big, curly-haired father. Catherine had retreated into polite mode. Miss Nice. Adam and Robert jostled together, struggled to dominate the conversation. Sometimes silence, then suddenly they both burst out talking at once. The same jabber and confusion inside Vinny. She kept forgetting which glass was for water and which for wine and holding out the wrong one to be refilled. Robert was noticing everything. Judging her. Vinny worried: did you tear bread or cut it? Were you allowed butter on bread in France? Did you eat pasta holding your fork in your right hand, like a spoon? She couldn't remember. The protocol mattered. A kind of magic spell, table manners. Get it right, the incantation, and it would let you escape unnoticed and unscathed. Elbows in, sit up straight, offer to pass the salt if you want it yourself. Then you became invisible.

Logs crackled and hissed behind her, and from time to time she turned round and glanced at the flames dancing in their cave of smoke-blackened stone. The burning lengths of sawn pine smelt resinous, sweet. Catherine was just toying with her lasagne, she saw, picking at the vegetable filling and pushing the rest aside. Pasta was fattening. Vinny rested her fork on her plate and hurled down some more wine. She didn't like it much. On her tongue it was warm and furry at first. Then came an aftertaste, thin like water, sharp, a hint of vinegar. The effect was useful, though. Blurriness, like a cotton-wool wall.

Robert's brown curls were burnished to gold in the harsh light cast by the bulb dangling overhead. The hairs on his forearms were golden too. He had rolled up his shirtsleeves and unbuttoned his collar as he warmed up. His face shone red with eating and drinking. He mopped up the last of his sauce with a piece of bread.

– Not much chance of a love affair with you around, young puritan, he said to Adam: you're delighted to say goodbye to all my girlfriends. You don't give them a chance.

– Most of them are stupid, that's why, Adam said.

Catherine kept her eyes on her plate, as though she were astonished people could talk this way in front of strangers. Vinny thought that that was the point: *épater* the little visiting *bourgeoises*, let them glimpse the true *vie de bohème*. She locked her feet around the legs of her chair, braced herself. She gulped mouthfuls of wine. Yet she was sure her face was a giveaway, pink and prim. She drained her glass, wincing as the acidity hit her stomach. Robert beckoned to Adam, jerking his chin towards the carafe. Obediently he poured them all more wine.

– The neighbours will approve, anyway, Robert said: no loose women sunbathing naked after the painting class and scandalising the postman. Poor Michel, do you know he believes in hell? He told me so last week while I was signing for a parcel.

Adam hesitated, then spoke hurriedly.

– Everybody here's a Catholic. It's not their fault. That's how they've been brought up. That's just the way they are.

– No, it was more than that, Robert said: it was some kind of threat, because I was in the middle of a painting and wouldn't let him into the studio to have a look.

Two small nudes decorated the wall opposite Vinny. Chalk pastels, pink and yellow smudged and rubbed together into flesh. Pneumatic women with tiny eyes, thighs swollen and tight like pork sausages. Luscious dolls who sprawled on divans, feet in the air as though they'd just fallen over. They had a comic and caricature air. Hapless girls with ridged gold curls and rosy cheeks.

– Madame Beauvin looked in the other day, Adam reproved his father: when she brought us those eggs, she wasn't shocked at all. She was interested.

– Yes, and whose fault was it she was let in? Robert retorted: yours.

Robert was obviously God up on a cloud surveying his creation, while the farmers round about were part of the background, tiny figures moving in a landscape like the peasants in a Nativity painting. He appreciated their being there; they rendered the countryside authentic; but their concerns were utterly remote from his. His son, on the other hand, he kept under close scrutiny, rapping out questions. Still messing about with live performances? Happenings or whatever you call them? Found a job yet? Just what d'you suppose you're going to live on? God forbid any child of mine becomes an artist! Get out there and make some money!

Adam hunched lower in his chair, scowling, eyes on his plate, and growled minimal responses. Vinny clenched her hands together in her lap. Adam turned to Catherine and asked her if she knew anything about gardening.

He had shown them around earlier. The property was enclosed by walls of greenery, evergreen hedges that had shot up and not been cut for years. Adam recited the names: box, privet, yew. The overgrown garden, curling away from the house along the brow of the slope, brimmed with bulky bushes you had to force a way between. Vinny jumped when the ground just in front of her suddenly fissured: a greybrown zigzag. A darting point of tongue; bunched scaliness that slithered out of the grass and lengthened, swift and sure; moved inexorably closer.

– It's OK, Adam reassured her: it's only a grass-snake.

Eventually she came to accept them. They wriggled to and fro, basked under bits of abandoned corrugated iron. If you disturbed them, for any reason, they undulated off, a muscular pour, rapid and alert. They had their own routes through the dandelions and thistles. The neglected garden belonged more to them, to the lizards and hedgehogs and toads, than to people. Its gravel paths had almost vanished under the grip of clover and couch. You made your own track through the nettles to find the end of the garden, past Robert's studio in the converted barn and through a tangle of elders, bramble and wild cherry. Here, where the copse petered out into a thicket of broom, the wooden posts of a fallen wire fence, half hidden in the undergrowth, marked the boundary where the garden became part of the forest.

Robert's studio, the former barn, was wide and lofty, towering above all the other buildings. Compared to it the low house and its dependent sheds were a mere huddle, clustered together like a sow and her piglets.

– The studio's kept locked, Adam explained: when Dad's not there. He doesn't like us going in when he's working, either.

Behind the house, reaching up the hill to the forest, was the field where the owners had presumably once grazed their cows. Nowadays rampant blackberries, coiling like barbed wire, barriers thrusting ten foot high, prevented you entering. Other fields close to the house, belonging to neighbouring farmers, were well tended: neatly fenced, stocked with apple trees, dotted with munching cows. By contrast, most of

Robert's land remained defiantly untended. He had cleared part of it, scything a patch of weed-filled grass to make a rough lawn, digging and planting a *potager* in the orchard in front of the house. But sorting out the studio had had to come first. He had happily abandoned the larger part of the garden, letting nature take it back, wreathe around and over it until it resembled the overgrown parterre in *Sleeping Beauty*.

The interior of the house was similarly like something out of a folk tale.

– Oh, it's lovely, Catherine said when she first entered it: I've never seen anything like this.

The *fermette* was the opposite of the small suburban house in which they had grown up. It had no carpets, curtains or chintz covers, no frills or decoration, few machines or gadgets. It was a play-house for children, a pretend version of the real thing. It reminded Vinny of all the camps she'd ever made in the garden shed or the coal-hole or the wasteland near the park. This was an undemanding structure, this artist's house, which apparently did not require to be daily attended to with dusters, hoovers, floor polishers, cans of beeswax, mops, carpet-cleaner, window-cleaner, lavatory-cleaner, bleach, bath-cleaner. As a result it shouldered a coat of dust, sported balls of grit and cobwebs in the corners, a thick layer of brown grease on the cooker. It wore this dishabille with a raffish and insouciant air.

– What a pity, Catherine whispered to Vinny: not to look after it a bit better. What a shame to let it get so dirty.

They were standing in the kitchen with Adam and Robert. A faint smell of mice hung in the air. The mottled blue and grey lino underfoot was grimy and sticky, dotted with crumbs and dead flies. The window was smeary, so that you couldn't see out of it, and the window-sill was piled with unwashed dishes. Robert, catching the criticism, shrugged.

– Feel free to clean up, darling, if you want to. I don't notice dirt, myself.

He flicked a glance at Catherine's shining hair, her ironed T-shirt and jeans, her unscuffed sandals. He waved them towards the back door.

– Adam can show you the bathroom. Such as it is. It's outside, through there.

On their second day Catherine asked Adam to drive her and Vinny into Sainte-Marthe, the local town.

– Would that be all right? Can you borrow your father's car?

– Of course, Adam said.

He was silent all the way into town. He drove fast along the narrow back roads, swearing when they met tractors coming the other way and he had to brake abruptly. Vinny was relieved when they entered Sainte-Marthe, joining a line of traffic snaking decorously past the *gendarmerie*, and had to slow down.

– You two go and sightsee or whatever, Catherine said: I've got some shopping to do.

– We'll meet here at the café in an hour's time, all right? Adam said.

Catherine waved, and darted off. Adam turned to Vinny.

– Come on, then.

He strode along with his hands in his pockets, frowning, tossing minimal explanations over his shoulder. He hustled Vinny past Sainte-Marthe's tourist attractions: the two streets of medieval houses, the *brocante*, the dolphin-adorned fountain in the main square, the war memorial, the covered market-place, and the basilica.

Pushing open the nail-studded side door of the basilica she re-entered her childhood. She paused in the nave, snuffing up the smell of damp stone and incense. Gothic vaults leaped towards each other high overhead. The paved floor was spattered with spots of coloured light. The enormous empty space bounded up, balanced fragile as eggshells, and the stained-glass windows tossed suns about like jugglers' toys.

An ugly modern altar had been set up on the near side of the choir stalls. An equally ugly crucifix dangled above it. She turned away quickly from these, preferring to dawdle with Adam along the curve of the apse, inspecting the side altars: a dead bishop in a glass case, a nineteenth-century booted and spurred Joan of Arc, nailed-up marble *ex-voto* tablets thanking Sainte Thérèse of Lisieux for her interventions.

– I haven't been into a church for years, Vinny said: though I was really into religion as a kid. Mass every Sunday, catechism classes, singing in the choir at school, the lot.

– Yeah, I remember, you told me that before, Adam said: I suppose I was luckier because I never had to go. Except at school. Dad's an atheist.

He yawned.

– Sorry, Vinny said: are you bored? Have you had enough? We can go now, if you like. I can always come back another time.

– One last chapel, Adam said: in here. It's the best one.

He opened a small leather-padded door in the wall to the left of the main altar and ushered Vinny through into the chill dimness beyond. This was a Romanesque chapel, small and crouched, its vault frescoed with a majestic Christ in Judgement outlined in red. One long forefinger upraised; angels with scrolled wings and arched bare feet surrounding him, two on each side, bearing him up. Beneath him, on a lace-covered stand, behind a black iron grille, a throned figure of the Virgin was surrounded by vases of pink and red gladioli. She was ramrod upright and straight under flowing pleats; balanced her miniature son on her left arm and raised her right hand, which held a tiny cup, in blessing. Her crown, garments and hands were coated in silver, as was her child. Her dark, unsilvered face was severe and remote. On the near side of the grille, tall thin candles were stuck on wire spikes in tiers; a grid of points of light. A handwritten notice instructed you what candles cost and where to put your money in the slot.

– She's called the Virgin of the Thorn, Adam explained: apparently a pilgrim was bringing some of her breast milk home from the Holy Land as a relic, but then he fell asleep under a bush, having hung the bag of milk on a branch, and when he woke up the bush had grown into a tree so that the bag of milk was out of reach, so he prayed to the Virgin and she bent the branch and he got the milk back. So the chapel was built to commemorate the miracle. That's how the story goes, anyway.

— What kind of bush? Vinny asked.

— A hawthorn, Adam said: they crop up in stories of visions all the time. They're magical bushes. Nearly always connected with the Virgin. Very powerful.

— For someone who was brought up an atheist, Vinny said: you know a lot about religious legends.

He blushed. She suddenly remembered that his mother had run away. Perhaps, irreligious as he was, he'd adopted this Virgin. Perhaps she symbolised a mother's continuing though invisible presence. One mother in the world who would never vanish, never fail you. She couldn't believe in that herself, but she was touched that perhaps Adam did.

— Sorry, she said.

— Stop apologising all the time, Adam snapped at her: it's really irritating.

Tears sprang into her eyes. She averted her face and began to inspect the large exercise book that lay open on a table next to the bank of lit candles. This proved to be a work by many authors, its ruled pages filled with painstakingly inscribed sentences in different varieties of the same hand, the round wobbly letters decorated with curlicues and flourishes. At first the writing was hard to read; quite different from the version she'd been taught in England.

Sainte Mère, *aidez-moi.*

Sainte Mère, *exaucez-moi*.

Sainte Mère, *priez pour moi*.

Detailed explanations of what was wrong; cries of need and anguish and suffering; all carefully traced in blue biro. A cheap plastic pen tethered by a length of string.

The Virgin stared sternly ahead. Vinny shivered.

Adam took her hand awkwardly.

– I had a bit of a row with Dad before coming out. He doesn't like me borrowing the car. It put me in a bad mood.

Why take it out on me? Vinny thought. But she saw this was the closest he could come to apologising. She followed him back to the sunshine outside, to the café where Catherine sat waiting, but not before she had hastily bought and lit a tall candle. For her intentions. Whatever those were.

– As though the Virgin put on her spectacles every night and read her correspondence, Catherine mused over icy lager: so sweet.

Catherine had headed for the *quincaillerie*. She displayed her purchases: a blue canvas apron, a wooden scrubbing brush and a bottle of Eau de Javel, a bunch of yellow dusters, a set of bowls and buckets, a dustpan and brush, a sponge.

That same afternoon she began cleaning, with Robert's amused permission. Vinny watched Robert studying them. Who were those two sisters in that French fairy tale? Rose Red and Snow White. One good and one bad. One feminine and one not. One kindly, pretty strawberry blonde who saw housework as an act of love, and one difficult gingernut tomboy who preferred to play outside. Was that the right story? No, Vinny shouted to herself: too simplistic, I refuse to be set against Catherine like that.

Catherine shrugged at Robert. She just got on with her self-appointed job and enjoyed herself, head turbaned in a tea-towel, apron tied over her skimpy shorts, transistor radio full on. Once the house had been scoured and mopped it was an easy place to keep clean: there was so little clutter in it. The furniture was simple, picked up cheap from farm sales: a long table and benches in the living-room, a smaller table in the kitchen, mattresses on metal spring bases in the rooms upstairs. Clothes were hung from hooks, pots and pans stored on shelves. There were no armchairs. French farmers didn't use them, Adam explained: the locals did all their socialising around the table. Instead, a half-moon of battered wicker garden chairs, packed with cushions, curved in front of the big stone fireplace.

Catherine plumped up the cushions every morning after she had swept the floor. She set jugs of buttercups, cow-parsley and Queen Anne's Lace here and there. She washed and ironed a blue and white checked cloth she found stuffed under the kitchen sink, scoured the rusted blades of the old black-handled knives, and laid the table carefully at night. She set out a group of candles stuck on saucers, arranged the prettiest and least chipped of the stack of old plates, and sliced the baguette into a basket she lined with a blue check handkerchief bought in the market.

Robert nodded to his guest over a tumbler of wine every

supper-time, toasting her: ah, that Catherine, she knows what she's about.

Catherine was almost curtseying and calling him kind sir. Mob-cap and stays for you, my girl. I'd have been the poacher, slinking through the moonlit garden with a rabbit in each pocket. Could I kill an animal? Dunno.

– The woman's touch, Vinny said: how to turn a house into a home.

– Shut up, Vinny, Adam said: leave her alone.

The house was constructed in thick-walled stone according to the most basic design, almost indistinguishable from the cattle sheds hunched alongside it. Only the former *pigeonnier* tower, which now housed the kitchen, gave it distinction. The crumbling façade had been crudely patched with cement. The small, shutterless windows were barred. Vinny did like the cool, dark interior, which was restful, and made sense in the summer heat. You could withdraw into it from the blistering sun outside. But she kept finding that rather than identify with the house, as Catherine did, caring for it, she had regularly to go out of it. She had to put some distance between herself and it. Then she could come back inside again. She preferred basking in the garden, letting the dazzling light warm her skin, probe her closed eyelids. The house was a shadowy cave, waiting. She could explore it if she wanted to. A puzzle of interlocking boxes, which might just spring traps. The middle attic with its thick cobwebs and owl droppings; the old bread-oven off the kitchen with its nests of grass-snakes; the damp, disused cellar littered with broken glass. You had to step warily near all of these.

The chief charm of the house consisted in its two staircases. One, on the left, as you entered, was a boxed-in semi-spiral of oak, rising up inside the stubby *pigeonnier* tower to reach the bedrooms that Robert had constructed, with Adam's help, in the former *grenier*. A makeshift conversion: white plasterboard walls hastily thrown up to divide the long space, one sloping-ceilinged room opening into the other, each lit by a single square pane of glass let into the roof. The end door in the first bedroom made a link into a central attic, which was crossed by a massive low beam. It had been left untouched because of its rotten floor, weakened by rain pouring in through a hole in the roof. The missing slates had been replaced, but then Robert's energy had run out.

For Vinny, peering in, this dark, abandoned space, as shadowy and mysterious as night, functioned as a memory of how the whole of the *grenier* must have formerly been: steeply pitched raftered ceiling showing the underside of the roof, bare unplastered stone walls, floorboards littered with straw, corners silted with grain husks. At the far side of this dusty loft, a door led into a second bedroom, which was reached from the garden by an exterior staircase. So in theory you could circle the house, going in and out, up and along and down.

You didn't do this, of course, because of the patch of rotten planks, which might give way beneath you, and because you didn't intrude into other people's bedrooms. Robert slept above the kitchen and Adam had the room at the far end. Spartan places, Vinny thought them when she was shown round: unpainted, with 1950s fluted glass lampshades dangling overhead, orange-boxes for cupboards, and ex-army blankets covering the low metal-sprung beds. It was a whim of Robert's, apparently, to rough it in France, to live as austerely as possible. No hot water, no heating other than the open fire. Robert never came here in winter. He was just playing at rusticity, Vinny thought. Poor people always longed for better conditions. She remembered her mother's delight when she got a proper washing-machine and no longer had to wind ropes of sheets through the mangle by hand.

– Where do the painting students sleep when they come? Catherine asked: surely there's not enough room for them?

– Oh, they go to the hotel in Sainte-Marthe, Adam said: except for the current favourite, of course.

Vinny and Catherine shared the guestroom, the former cowshed under Adam's room. The walls had been whitewashed, long ago, and were still hung with grain sieves, coils of rope, halters, and bits of old harness. The cowshed had a wooden ceiling formed by the underneath of the floorboards above, a combed concrete floor. Furniture was an iron double bed, and a manger in which they stored their clothes. A small uncurtained window in a deep stone recess let in a little daylight. On this ledge Catherine put a jam jar of flowering purple mint pulled from the ditch in the lane. She brushed the thick cobwebs off the walls, sluiced the floor, hung their bead necklaces from a nail on the back of the wide wooden door. This swung open on to the grass. It was easy for Vinny to slip out, up the stairs, and into Adam's room. At night the garden was cold and damp, threaded through with the shivery calls of owls.

On that first evening, Catherine was brisk about going to bed early and sending Vinny up to join Adam. Vinny wasn't even sure she wanted to go. The converted cowshed looked so snug. A lamp enclosing a stub of candle hung from a hook in the wall just above the bed, casting a pool of golden light edged by black shadow.

– Sure you'll be all right down here on your own? Vinny asked.

Catherine was wearing her pink cardigan over the 1930s crêpe-de-Chine nightdress Vinny had given her last Christmas. She was curled up against a bank of pillows and cushions, reading an old book of recipes she had found in the kitchen, an olive green blanket pulled around her. She looked up and pursed her mouth. She flicked one hand dismissively.

How black the night was, outside. Vinny, her Afghan waistcoat clutched on over her kimono, blundered, torchless, to the woodshed turned bathroom. Ivy tendrils thrust through a crack in the stone wall and twined about the blotched mirror. A stencilled Chinese tin bowl and jug stood on a slab of cracked marble. You filled these from a tap outside. The lavatory, smelling of chemicals, was like an oil drum, with a thin wooden seat. Damn. She had forgotten her toothbrush and toothpaste, which she'd packed in her shoulder-bag. She'd slung this from her chair at table and left it behind. She would have to go back indoors and fetch it.

She went out again, surer-footed this time, into the dewy garden. It smelt of fresh earth and cows. No stars. No moon.

The front door was unlocked. It scraped as she pushed it open. The room was melted to darkness, except for the red glow of the fire. Though the leaping flames of earlier on had died down, half a charred log still smouldered on top of a heap of ashes, the top layer twinkling red.

The collapsed fire cast enough light to illuminate the late-night visitor. A middle-aged woman wearing a long blue linen dress. She looked up as Vinny pushed in. She was sitting with her bare feet propped on the hearth, her hands folded over a couple of books in her lap. She had short hair dyed dark auburn. Her gaze was surprised and intent. Presumably one of the neighbours. Perhaps the Madame Beauvin who'd been talked of earlier.

– Oh, excuse me, Vinny said in her best, careful French: I just came in to fetch my bag. I left it in here earlier on.

The woman nodded at her in a friendly way. Vinny spotted her bag just where she'd left it, suspended from the back of a chair. She picked it up.

– Bonsoir, Madame.

The woman nodded again. Vinny went out.

She skipped cleaning her teeth and ran up the stairs to Adam's bedroom. She knocked, breathless, at his door.

He was lying in bed just as Catherine had, curled up

around a book; defended and closed-off. Then he threw down the book.

— You look all pink, he said, studying her: are you all right?

Vinny stripped off her clothes and let them drop. In a few moments she was under the blankets with him, arms round him, head on his shoulder. Either he knew Robert had a visitor or he didn't. It wasn't her business.

They turned their faces towards each other and kissed. Adam hadn't cleaned his teeth either. He tasted of wine and olive oil. What a mouth he had for kissing, her sweetheart, her milk and honey boy. What a beauty he was, so fierce and soft, so furred, so thin. She could feel his ribs under her hands. The bones of his pelvis pressed into her. She tugged his curls, his ears. The hollow of his collarbone tasted of salt. He held her so tightly he nearly squeezed the breath out of her. She kissed the line of hair that ran down his stomach. His hands stroked her waist and back until she felt she could die from joy.

When they shambled downstairs in the morning the house was hushed. Robert was already ensconced in his studio. Vinny soon learned his routine. He got up early to work. He vanished after his solitary breakfast, carrying off bread, ham and cider for lunch, and reappeared at dinner. Sometimes he disappeared into the forest on solitary walks, clambering around the rocks on the summit of the hill. This rocky place, littered with granite slabs, was called the Devil's Table.

— Can we go and see it? Vinny asked, swigging coffee.

She and Adam were sitting on the front steps in the

sunshine. Catherine sprawled in a ragged deckchair nearby, nibbling a peach. The other two feasted on crusty lengths of bread covered with slabs of cold butter and dollops of apricot jam.

– Sure, if you want to, Adam said: well, according to Madame Beauvin anyway, witches used to meet there for human sacrifice.

Vinny decided not to mention that Madame Beauvin had been in the house the night before.

– Creepy, Catherine said.

– Lots of caves up there, Adam said: tunnels all through the hillside, apparently.

They were sitting so close together that Vinny could drink in the smell of his skin. She felt contented as a cat full of milk. Last night she'd had her first orgasm with him. He was the first lover with whom that had happened. She'd had them on her own for years, but never with a man so far. She'd been a slow starter. Other boyfriends had lost patience with her and gone off. Am I frigid? she'd fretted to Catherine. Don't be daft, Catherine had replied. Adam's curiosity, wanting to find out what she was like, made her feel able to be honest as well as passionate, telling him. Please do this. Yes, I like that. They'd shifted and fingered and nudged for weeks, then suddenly, last night, here in Adam's room in France, they got the knack; it happened. Something to do with the way that Adam didn't just retire into himself, fling himself at her, use her for his own pleasure then fall asleep. He remembered who she was and looked into her eyes as they fucked.

That was so powerful you could almost feel afraid. Trust and confidence made her come. You desired, you moved the way you needed to, you concentrated, you didn't stop, and bingo.

Vinny, coming, had shouted out: I love you I love you I love you. She was so enraptured by her discovery that she could do it that she had wanted to make love again immediately; all night. Adam had protested sleepily. No. So now, this morning, she felt awkward as well as happy, that she'd been too demanding, that she ought to hold herself back, slow down, take his rhythm as her own.

It became their joke, at first, how often Vinny wanted to make love. How much she wanted of everything. Food wine cigarettes sunshine sleep dope sex. Certainly there was an extra frisson of pleasure from having sex out here, away from home in a foreign country, in this languor-inducing heat. Night after night she slid up the outside stone staircase, pinned Adam down on the bed, and caressed him until he gave in. When she came, he put his hand over her mouth to muffle her cries. When they made love in the daytime he veiled his room with music from his transistor radio.

Robert also used music to create private space. You could tell when he was in his studio because he had the radio on loud, a reminder to them to keep well away while he concentrated on a painting. He was the only one who worked. The other three were unashamedly on holiday. Often Catherine wandered off, tactfully leaving the other two alone, smiling, saying she was bored with their company or with the conversation; she'd go and find something else to do.

Sometimes she stayed. The three of them were comfortable together, talking idly, sunbathing, lying face down in the grass blank with heat, arguing about whose turn it was to go and fetch some more cold beers from the fridge. Vinny brimmed with happiness. Here she was, with her two best-beloveds. So close. They made a circle that held love. Like a fountain arching up in sunlight, endlessly replenished, end-lessly running over.

The time in summer was different from normal time. It stretched according to whim. The long days, free of schedules or imposed organisation, brought indolence. They could sleep late, loll in deckchairs all afternoon reading, raid the vegetable garden when they got hungry. Adam fetched the bread every morning from the bakery in Sainte-Madeleine, on his bicycle, sometimes taking Vinny with him on another old bone-shaker dug out from a storeroom. Robert went into town in the car once a week to do the shopping. Often Catherine went with him, so that she could force him to accept some housekeeping money from her and Vinny. They all ate together every night, and took turns cooking.

Vinny had never drunk so much wine before. It accounted for their lethargy in the mornings, their sloth in the after-noon. At night, at supper, fired up by the wine, they talked and argued. Once Vinny mentioned women's liberation but Robert interrupted her, laughing.

– I met this feminist chick in London. God, she was scary. Dressed in black leather and riding a motorbike.

– I'm a feminist, Vinny said.

– Not like her you're not. This chick, she was a real feminist all right. Kill you as soon as look at you.

He leaned across and stroked Vinny's cheek. She was sitting next to him. She could see the golden hairs on his chest. His brown face was creased up with amusement. Adam frowned. Robert saw the frown, and smiled more broadly. He elaborated. Women's liberation, now he stopped to think about it, was just a part of sexual freedom. This was a subject he liked to thunder about. He teased the scowling Adam with tales of his exploits, listed the names of sophisticated sexual positions that various girlfriends had enjoyed, quoted from Henry Miller and de Sade and Georges Bataille, scattered porn mags across the bathroom floor. Adam shrugged and remained silent. Catherine was a good child of the sixties, determined to be sturdily unshockable. She humoured Robert. Vinny boiled with resentment, which she tried not to show. He was Adam's father, after all, and she was a guest in his house. He seemed to like her. He was always giving her bear-hugs; kisses. He called her darling little Miss Puritan-Prig-Prude-Prim. Sometimes she drank enough wine for her discomfort to spill out, incoherent and messy, like vomit on the tablecloth. Adam would watch her miserably as she tried to explain to Robert why he should not define women's freedom in masculine terms. She failed every time.

Afterwards Catherine would soothe her: what's the point in freaking out? People should be able to express whatever they feel. You shouldn't try and censor them. You're so intolerant.

Sooner or later Adam would square up to his father, and the two of them would indulge in their own passionate disagreements about art or politics. These easily led to rows. They knew exactly how to wind each other up to the point of explosion, the threat of physical violence. Then whoever was angrier, Adam or Robert, would storm off and stamp around the garden.

These flare-ups died down by the following day. Catherine refused to be intimidated by them. She said they were just part of Robert's game. Vinny would swig too much red wine and fret. After a confrontation with Robert Adam never wanted to make love. Yet she wanted him to stand up to his father. She wanted to do so herself. The cost of fighting, though, was loneliness. When Adam turned away from her in bed, after a row at suppertime, she was stricken to the heart, as though he'd actually hit her. His remoteness made him seem a robot, polite and dead-eyed, his soul flown somewhere else. She told herself he couldn't help his coldness. He wasn't in control of his responses. But nonetheless, when he wouldn't talk to her, pushed her away, she found it hard not to feel like a wounded child, not to become tearful, demanding. At these times, Catherine, and the room they shared, became her refuge. Catherine was so wise. She was calm, a freckled brown Madonna.

– Leave him alone for a bit. Give him some space. Men hate clingy women.

For a month life went on in this way. Then, the pattern changed. Robert finished a big painting. He had been thinking about it for months and had suddenly been able to complete it in a matter of weeks. He locked it away in the storeroom.

– Can't we see the picture? Vinny asked.

– Not yet, Robert said: one day, sweetie, maybe.

Now he had some free time, a breathing-space.

– Come on, you lazy sod, he said to Adam: time you started giving me a hand with the garden.

They began working together in the afternoons, up behind the house, in the overgrown field that rose in a gentle slope above the stone-built cattle sheds. The plan was first to clear the ground roughly, advancing into the tight thickets of thorns with long-handled scythes, and then to decide on what wild saplings to leave and what to cut down. They barred their house guests from helping, from entering the field at all.

– We want it to be a surprise, Adam said: you can't see it until it's finished.

Catherine's birthday was approaching, and the night of the full moon. They planned a celebration: a supper party in the new garden space, a trestle table carried up, lanterns hung in the trees, and fireworks. Vinny volunteered to do the cooking, Adam to see to the music and decorations. Catherine tried to look cool, but she could not help preening with delight. She hennaed her hair, painted her toenails silver, and started cutting up two of her dresses to make a new patchwork one. Blue and yellow squares overstitched with gold braid. She got Vinny to tack the full gathers on to the waistband. They sat on the doorstep, sewing and drinking beer.

After a week of labour, Adam and Robert wanted some recognition of what they'd achieved so far. They invited the women up one heavy grey afternoon.

You entered the field by a stone staircase built at the side of the farthest shed to the left of the house. Stone wall on one side, tightly wound and prickly hedgerow on the other. Now this entrance had been cleared. You no longer had to stoop, force your way up through overhanging holly and hazel. What had been a tunnel was now an opening, a rosebush revealed on one side and a vine, trained against the side of the shed, on the other. The stairs themselves had been scraped clean of drifts of dead leaves, crusts of moss. The two women stood on the top step and looked about.

A spread of green. No longer a neglected and overgrown field. This wild place had become a meadow once more, its edges clearly visible. It was surrounded by a low earth bank supporting a mixture of hedgerow and trees. Behind these you could see moving friezes of cows, black and white. Adam and Robert waved to them from the far end.

Vinny vividly remembered the impenetrable wilderness of thorny bushes that had been here previously. The two men had removed it, sheared it away like a sheep's coat, yet it remained clearly in her memory. Her mind's eye superimposed the one image over the other. Most of the brambles were gone, the self-seeded oak and chestnut saplings uprooted, the tides of tall ferns, thistles and nettles slashed.

All had been consumed in a great bonfire. A circle of grey ash, still smouldering, marked the spot. Now old fruit trees were revealed, freed from their strangling wrappings, the long sprays of spiky bramble stems torn from their branches. She and Catherine walked up to the trees, around them. Touching the trunks, gnarled, covered with moss. Adam came across and told them the names. Apple and pear, cherry and peach. A walnut tree. A fig. Four ancient cider-apple trees, so bent they looked as though they were about to fall over. The small red fruits were round and hard as rosy beads.

– It's not a meadow at all, is it? Vinny said: it's a second orchard. How extraordinary you didn't know it was here.

– One of the neighbours would probably have told us, Adam said: if we'd asked.

He wandered back to work. He and Robert were almost finished. They were cutting their way around the under-growth at the field's circumference, chopping down the wild broom, the remaining tangles of brambles and screens of waist-high ferns, thinning the tall hazel hedge to let in more light. They had revealed treasures: a wild rose, long loops of bryony and honeysuckle, clumps of papery-flowered hon-esty. They had chucked down lofty ramparts of debris alongside them as they went, so that they seemed to be work-ing in a ditch, the bank on one side and the cut stuff on the other.

– Can we help? Catherine shouted.

– You can clear this lot up, Robert shouted back.

Vinny followed Catherine across the field. They found the

rakes and pitchforks leaning against the walnut tree and worked out what to do with them. Gather the fallen vegetation into tall heaps, then fork it up and carry it over to the fire. Rake up all the cut fern stalks out of the grass and shift these over too.

Raking was much harder work than Vinny expected. Soon her arms began to ache. Sweat dripped down her face, and she felt her cheeks grow crimson. Nonetheless there was a fierce pleasure in digging the long tines of the fork into a heap of branches, hoisting it high above her head and walking it down the meadow to where Catherine was already lighting the fire. She had never used a pitchfork. She was surprised at what a great mass of leafy rubbish you could pick up in one go.

– Birnham Wood, she shouted to Adam, but he had his back turned and didn't hear.

The sawn-up wild broom and fir trees had to be dealt with by hand. They dragged the spiky branches, coiled with long trails of blackberry sprays, down the meadow, one by one. Carried the heavier logs between them. They picked a handful of blackberries each, just to try them, smearing the backs of their juice-stained hands against their mouths to wipe off the stickiness. Some were watery, others fat and sweet.

The long tangles of brambles were hard to get a grip on, surprisingly heavy to lift. Since they'd been left where they fell, not laid in manageable heaps, they clung together in enormous masses that had to be dragged apart. Just when you thought you'd got a bunch of them sorted, snared and coiled on your fork, ends tucked in, they whipped back and caught your skin. Catherine and Vinny swore as the thorns ripped their arms and lines of blood spurted. They went doggedly on, hauling the springy bundles into basket-like meshes to be jabbed, swung up over their heads, marched to the fire.

The dry ferns went on first in lacy brown layers. On top of these they laid the lopped branches of the hazel, the broom, the fir, the ornamental pine. These were oozing resin, which made the fire catch and burn well. Scarlet flames, very clear in the sunlight, leaped up. They all stood around to watch, Catherine and Vinny leaning on their rakes. Aromatic smoke gushed up, smelling like the incense in the basilica.

The blood pumped in Vinny's face. She felt solid and furry with heat. If only she could cool down. But although it was late afternoon it was still hot and humid. The sky was covered over with grey clouds.

– Thundery, Robert said: good to get rid of this lot before the rain comes.

He glanced at Vinny.

– You look hot.

He looked amused at her disarray. She felt so cross she gathered up her courage.

– It would have been a lot easier getting the brambles over here if you and Adam had chucked them down into heaps. It's much harder to lift them when they're all tangled up in huge long masses.

Robert laughed.

– Bit late now. You've done it all, my little Amazon.

He threw on more armfuls of dead nettles and thistles, more fragrant fans of green spikiness. The fire was like a violent red mouth. It ate greedily whatever they gave it. Branches, short logs, green weeds. It snapped and hissed, licking sap off its lips. The flames shot up, died down, shot up again. They tended it with the rakes, throwing fallen parts back on, pushing embers together, poking and stirring it. Some of this fiddling was unnecessary, but it was enjoyable. Vinny smacked the heaped brambles with her pitchfork, forcing them down on to the flames. Inside herself she glowed with scarlet cinders. She wanted to flame out, and so she smacked again at the pile of crisp brown stalks, sending up showers of sparks.

Adam went back to the house and reappeared with the big, two-handled laundry basket packed with small bottles of beer, a big bottle of cider, some tumblers.

– Might as well make a party of it.

He'd brought an umbrella too, which Catherine opened and spun above her like a sunshade. Then she closed it and drove its spike into the ground.

What were they celebrating? Vinny felt it must be the end of summer, the toppling ripeness of the season, the hazelnuts and apples clustering on the trees, the red berries gleaming on the bryony and hawthorn in the hedgerow. The bonfire with its freight of killed greenery made her feel sad, and yet it was beautiful too. Sweat rinsed her back. It felt good now to stand around in the heat; wearing only a skimpy voile top and denim hotpants; tasting the warm bitterness of the beer as it slid down, breathing in the bitter smell of burning, the scent of grass and freshly cut pine, watching the plumes of smoke, the red flames flicker up like antlers.

The branches on the top of the bonfire were dark, heaped up in the rough shape of a star. Underneath them now was a disc of thick white ash. A dark star on snowy white, grey smoke billowing out as a breeze blew up, flakes of silvery ash dancing sideways, the red jiggle of fire above. Her cheeks burned; cool air swished over her bare shoulders. She tilted her bottle of beer. Froth, and the last few drops.

Robert threw down his scythe.

– That's it for me. I'm off back to the studio. See you later.

He patted Vinny on the shoulder. Then he dropped his empty beer bottle into the basket and walked off towards the steps.

– We'll make supper tonight, Catherine called after him.

He waved a hand above his head.

– Good girl.

Vinny didn't want to go back indoors. She wanted to catch the very last of the light before it began to rain; to go on looking at the fire. So when the other two began collecting up the saw, the rakes and pitchforks, the scythes, she didn't help them. She up-ended the heavy wicker basket, tipping the remaining bottles out into the grass, and sat down on it.

– What shall we cook? Catherine asked Adam.

– Dunno, he said: suppose we could dig up the last of the spinach. See what else there is.

– Eggs, too, Catherine was musing: and I'll make a big salad. I'll come with you and pick some herbs and a lettuce.

– I'll watch the fire a bit longer, Vinny said: just to make sure it burns down properly.

– I'll leave you the umbrella, Adam said: I think you'll need it.

He touched her shoulder, as Robert had, in parting. Her crossness flowed off her with her sweat. She sat there dreamily. Their voices died away behind the house and she began to feel the quiet. The fire was a big seething mass of red. When heavy drops fell on her neck and arms she put up the blue and white striped umbrella. She enjoyed hunching in her solitary bubble with rain splashing all round her. She didn't feel cold at all. The fire burned on even as the rain made the ash sizzle. Now the meadow was lush, its green carpet of weeds drinking up the wet. The curled heads of sprouting ferns were loaded with water.

After ten minutes the rain stopped. The grey clouds parted and flew away, revealing a pale blue sky. The sun flashed out, golden and low; she could just see it through a gap in the hedgerow trees. Beams of sun entered the meadow like swords, striking the ground with light. Glittering raindrops filled the cups of hazel leaves, fringed every blade of grass.

The sun has dipped, gone. A few clouds return, rounded puffs of apricot, rose. The far roofs of the Beauvins' farm glow pink, and the field in front of them, and the hills just behind. A pigeon starts calling in the wood, its mate cooing back. The fire fizzes. Crickets rasp nearby. Very faintly, the sound of the church bells ringing in the village blows across the field. Vinny dawdles on. Half an hour? An hour? Time doesn't matter. She is just here. She doesn't have to do anything, just sit on her improvised stool and be part of the golden evening, chin propped on hands, wet grass touching her bare ankles. She's not Vinny any more she's grass light earth she's the hedge the water the trees she's all of them she's purest happiness.

The lowing of cows somewhere nearby, a woman's voice shouting, breaks her trance. She gets up and goes indoors, yawning, lugging the basket and the umbrella. She blinks and stumbles in the kitchen doorway because it seems so dark in here.

She makes extra fuss and noise, a warning for the shadow over by the stove to break itself in half. Cathadam Cathadam break it up you two. She's fumbling with the door-latch, dropping a beer bottle. Chattering loudly and exclaiming. Anything to give them time. To give herself time. To save Catherine and Adam from knowing she has seen.

It's not happening and there is no need to get upset.

Get out of here.

Vinny blunders from the house, across the path to the gate, into the lane dipping steeply downhill. The ground is muddy and slippery after the recent rain, but she doesn't watch where she's going, doesn't care if she slips and slithers. She'd like to fall over, so that she could bawl like a baby.

Then someone might come and rescue her. Be kind. Make everything better. Make time turn back.

Round the corner she stumbles into a herd of cows. They surround her, bulky creatures tossing up their horned heads in surprise, snorting warm breath at her, trampling and mooing. Of course. Milking time is over. The cows are coming back from the farm. It takes her a few moments to realise that the young woman with short black hair, armed with a stick, who is marshalling the animals, is calling to her. Just as though she were a disobedient calf.

– Stay still. Stay still. Or you'll frighten them.

How enormous these beasts are, close to. As tall as she is. Furry coats, big eyes. The cows flow past, towards their field, shamble in, udders swaying loose, through the open gate. The young woman slaps it shut behind the last of them, secures it with a loop of wire. She turns to Vinny and nods at her.

– Hello. You're one of my English neighbours, aren't you? My name is Jeanne Beauvin.

Vinny is hanging her head and snivelling, wiping her nose on her forearm. She raises her head and stares. Madame Beauvin is young. Who was that other one, then?

Her newly met neighbour advances on her briskly. They shake hands.

– Come and see my house, says Jeanne Beauvin: I would like to show you my house.

PART NINE

Memories both sustain and torment me, dear master. Memories of that first year Emily and I were pupils together at your school.

When you looked in at the door the dormitory seemed to stretch away into infinite space. It was filled with floaty lengths of pale cotton like rustling wings. These were the curtains surrounding the boarders' beds. In the daytime pulled back and furled neatly, to open the bed, the chair and the tiny chest of drawers to Madame's inspection, and at night flurried round each pupil as she got undressed, knelt to say her prayers, climbed in between the sheets.

From the door, in the daytime, the dormitory was clean, silent, spacious. At mid-morning a forbidden space, unreachable as heaven, hovering at the top of three curving flights of stairs. Pretending not to know you, that you never went in there, that it was untouchable and untouched. At night it was crowded with bodies like a railway station, people in a waiting-room giving up all hope of their train's arrival, flinging themselves down anywhere to pass out. The school was a machine that turned out nice *jeunes filles* and the dormitory combed them into rows, ready for next day's grind and push.

The white cotton veil around your bed separated your dreams from those of your companions on either side. Groans and murmurs as girls restlessly dozed; the smell of soap, urine, sweaty armpits and feet; and your self nearly extinguished by the weight of so many other sleepers pressing in all around you.

Madame Heger gave Emily and me cubicles next to one another, at the far end. If I awoke in the night I listened for my sister's breathing close to mine. I knew immediately if she had left her bed and gone wandering. The air sagged empty. I would pull on my dressing-gown, thrust my feet into slippers, and pursue her into the dark. She might come to harm. The dormitory door creaked open under my fearful hand. I fled softly down the shadowy corridor, in and out of shafts of moonlight piercing the uncurtained windows, my felt soles sliding on the tiled floor. She might be in the classroom, hunting for a book, or strolling in the oratory, flicking her fingernail over the carved backs of prie-dieux, or in the kitchen, foraging in the larder for leftover supper scraps. If I found her I could join her. That was her rule for that game. Once, we climbed out of a skylight on to the flat edge of the roof, perched swinging our legs above the gutters, shared filched slices of redcurrant tart. Emily liked to pretend, sometimes, that we were still ten years old. Why not? Girls and boys come out to play the moon doth shine as bright as day.

We stole extra time for ourselves to persuade each other that we were somehow special, that we did matter. Too many girls in that school, uniform in drab dark dresses and white collars, like nuns, and we wanted to stand out, for one another at least. I depended upon Emily to look back at me and remind me that I was myself. This was a burden for her, I daresay. I didn't let myself imagine that it was me she was escaping at night; that, in her turn, she needed to feel utterly free, even of me.

The other pupils saw us as the spoilt foreign girls. You had a little troupe of favourites who clustered adoringly around your estrade after class, hung about in doorways to watch you pass, blushed and turned away, giggling, when you caught their gaze. You did distinguish us among those nincompoops, Monsieur. To Emily you remarked that she might make a great navigator, and to me you indicated that I had a certain facility for storytelling. Once I'd learned to control my over-exuberant style, to prune ruthlessly, to keep my imagination checked within bounds.

Madame Heger watched all the schoolgirl simperings and oglings indulgently. It was she whom you went to bed with every night, after all. She could afford to indulge your need for favourites and flatterers; your need to flirt. She approved of us too; at the beginning, anyway. Odd little English students in their ugly, outlandish clothes. Charlotte's accent is really improving, she would declare. And Emily shows a most pleasing willingness to learn.

But then there began a period when I could not find Emily at night at all. She vanished from the dormitory in the few moments it took me to feel her absence and waken properly. She disappeared into the shadows. I hunted her in vain. I suppose I clung to her too much. She needed to shake me off. She must have felt she had to be brutal or she would never have had a moment to herself. In the morning she'd watch me through a slit in the bed-hangings, out of the corner of her eye, enjoying her triumph. Silly old Char. You can't catch me.

I tracked her down by imagining where I would most like to go myself. The answer was obvious.

That house was a complete world; an entire geography. It was divided in two. One half was dark, and the other light. One half was plainly furnished. The other boasted vases of flowers, pictures in gilt frames, velvet cushions, sofas. Softness and glitter and perfumes belonged to your half of the house, Monsieur. All Madame Heger's taste, which Emily and I despised as showy and flash. Everything of hers was decorated, wrapped in lace, hung with tassels. We preferred your study, which we had peeped at on our first day, exploring the place, before we learned about the dividing line, beyond which we must not go.

The study was your sanctum and bolt-hole, because it was your library. You had an entire roomful of books all to yourself. New ones, bought from the bookseller two streets away, stacked in piles on the table, smelling freshly of ink and leather, the pages uncut, awaiting your paper-knife to slice them apart and reveal their contents. Not schoolbooks such as we had to be content with, inky and battered, covered in fresh coats of brown paper at the start of every term, passed on from pupil to pupil then collected back in. Your books, neatly bound in half-calf, titles in gold leaf stamped on the spines, and your name flowingly inscribed on the flyleaf, belonged to you and no-one else.

Your study was scented with your cigars, with your pipe tobacco. A rich smell that curled into one's heart and stomach. Intoxicating as the warm smell of earth in spring. I loved your smell.

From bed to book. From dormitory to library. That was Emily's preferred trajectory. And then mine too. I crept after her. I listened outside your door and heard your two voices plaiting happily together. You didn't always go to bed at the same time as Madame Heger. Sometimes you sat up late, by yourself, reading. You allowed Emily in, pretending she was still a child, just a pupil who couldn't sleep, a homesick girl, far away from her family, in need of comfort and reassurance, some words of advice. And then, since you discovered what a clever girl she was, how intelligent, how talented at translation and composition, you began to take pleasure in talking to her. You allowed her to stay up longer each time. You let her curl up in the armchair opposite you, bare feet tucked under a cushion, and stare at you with her big eyes, and talk to you of books. While I shivered in the passageway outside and clenched my fists until the nails dug into the palms of my hands.

That's how I knew I wasn't dreaming. Not making it all up. Waking in the morning and seeing the red dents and scratches on my hands.

PART TEN

When she got back from her summer holiday Vinny was broke. Her former job at the charity had finished. Dully she went out and got another one. Practical problems could supersede emotional ones. When she remembered, she winced, then felt raw, untouchable, as though her arms had been torn off. Her stomach seemed to have been torn out too. She couldn't eat; she drank and smoked instead. She supposed she was angry with Adam and Catherine, who had stayed on in France, but habits of love died hard; she missed them as well. They were the ones who knew her best. She ached for their comfort; as though, having punched a hole in her, they could mend her too. She had brought back with her some postcards of Loire valley châteaux, since she had found none of Sainte-Madeleine in the local tabac, and she imagined writing them one. Beautiful weather – having a terrible time – think my heart is broken – wish I weren't here – love and kisses. That was it: she wanted them to feel guilty. Anger was too much to cope with just now. She felt it settling on her skin like rust.

In London you could vanish among the other walking wounded on the street. Vinny sat for hours in her local at

Mile End, crouched over glasses of Guinness. She reread *Jane Eyre*, comforted because Jane was so fierce. Cast out from belonging anywhere, a homeless wanderer who had to beg for food and sleep rough, she claimed the moon for mother and fought to survive. Turning the pages, Vinny licked creamy froth off her lips. She always drank pints, defying the barman, who thought them unladylike. Vinny compounded the insult by smoking roll-ups and not smiling. John the barman considered her, unmade-up, wearing scruffy clothes and drinking alone without a male chaperon, to be a supercilious middle-class show-off, probably a dyke. The women who drank in his pub always looked nice, because it was a treat to get out and they dressed accordingly, and they were accompanied by their husbands or boyfriends. They could be placed as decent; slotted in as good. Unlikely to kick up rows or fuss when men teased them; able to give as good as they got; of course that made them preferable as customers. He knew them all and had their respect. But since Vinny had got to know some of these women regulars, and was tolerated by them, John was forced to put up with her. He watched sardonically when, assuming Vinny was very poor, they shyly presented her with items of their daughters' cast-off clothes, tactfully wrapped up in brown-paper parcels.

Early Sunday lunchtimes were her favourite: the emptiness and quiet; the door of the public bar propped open letting in the light; the planked floor, newly scoured, smelling of soap. Her drink finished, Vinny would get on her bike, which she had left chained to the railings outside, and go for a ride along the canal out towards Hackney Marshes. The distant tower blocks, sparkling in the sun, looked like giant batteries. She wheeled over muddy sand, past clumps of wild Michaelmas daisies and rosebay willowherb in prodigal flower. The abandoned factories looked very white. The canal smelt of weed and rot and petrol. Something saltier, too, which made you feel the river was nearby, and suggested the memory of the sea, which Vinny had crossed by herself, coming back, fleeing to this inner-city landscape which let you pull itself over your head like a thick scarf. Green images of the French countryside receded, streaks of paint on a distant brick wall.

In their place came memories. She was parted from her childhood shared with Catherine; across a sea of pain. When she called for her sister a mocking voice replied. Catherine shortening her name from Delphine to Finny. Then Vinny. Then, sometimes, Vin. Vin *de table*, Catherine labelled her: Vin *ordinaire*. Only Vinny was allowed to call her elder sister Cath. She tracked her through school, borrowed her green eye-shadow without asking, tried on her stiletto heels. Stop copying me, Catherine complained, but Vinny copied everything that Catherine did, from buying jeans that zipped up at the front and not at the side to insisting on letting her hair grow and putting it in rollers at night. A Formica-clad salon in Stanmore was where her mother had taken Catherine and herself for haircuts, all through their adolescence. An old Polish man with a grey, exquisitely mounded coiffure. Mr Lecky, that was it. Could that have really been his name?

Perhaps he'd changed it, in order to fit in. He was a Catholic, which was why they went to him. He wore a hip-length grey nylon jacket, from whose breast-pocket poked a pair of scissors, a grey comb. He smelt of sweet aftershave, which clashed with the scent of hairspray. He gave them savage short cuts with square fringes and flirted with their mother. Pink-cheeked, she lapped up his compliments. The two girls wriggled and scowled. At the age of sixteen Catherine had rebelled against Mr Lecky and insisted on growing her hair. He was permitted to shave half an inch off the ends twice a year; no more. Vinny had rapidly followed suit, to Catherine's disgust. Then in her early twenties Vinny went out and got a crew-cut. She'd been the first to rebel. She was also the first to get pregnant and the first to have an abortion. The abortion clinic was in Stanmore, not far from Mr Lecky's shop. Did he know there was an abortion clinic close by? Presumably not. Mr Lecky's scissors could stab Catherine in the belly, the heart. Would Catherine have a child with Adam? Vinny thought so. She didn't tell either of them about her abortion. There was no point.

On the evening of her return from the clinic she went to the pub and drank whisky. At home, sodden with drink, she slumped into sleep. She dreamed she was a library housing many books printed in invisible ink; stories of women that nobody wanted to read. The library would have to be burned down. Vinny was the arsonist. She set fire to herself and smelt her flesh begin to roast; greasy, and blackening. She heard it sizzle.

PART ELEVEN

You don't know the true nature of my departure, Monsieur. That's because you never bothered to find out.

You don't know what goes on when your back is turned; when you go away. You imagine, I daresay, that the rituals of domestic life continue as normal: Monsieur's shirts must be washed and pressed, his boots blacked, his bookshelves dusted; fair copies of his manuscripts made; against his return. The house revolves; stops; revolves again. The music-box is wound up and plays. The pigeons coo in the *allées* in the garden. The cabbages in the vegetable plot grow in the straightest possible lines.

Of course you like to get out of the house and enjoy a little freedom, a little wildness, from time to time. Every so often you grow bored with ruling over fifty adoring students, a sedate compliant wife, your well-behaved children. It's too easy to command their devotion, their admiration; just as it was too easy to command mine. A man needs change; a little salt instead of this diet of sweetmeats. Off you hop for fresh stimulus elsewhere and who can blame you? Too much worship drives a man mad. You need new battles to fight; new territories to conquer. New disciples to impress.

How bitter you have grown, Charlotte, I hear you say. Certainly I have, Monsieur. I have lost any trace of sweetness I once had. It melted away with too much crying and I'm all the better for it: scrubbed clean of sentimental hope; rinsed of delusion.

She waits, my dear Monsieur, that lovely wife of yours, until you're absent for several days, away on a lecture tour. Then she seizes me. When you return, she'll say that a telegram arrived, summoning me urgently home to England. I've gone. I left you my best regards, my thanks for your many kindnesses, and said goodbye. When, later, a letter fails to come from Haworth, thanking you again for all you did for me, she'll shrug. *Mal-élevée*. I always said so, *mon cher* Constantin.

I'll die here and you'll never know. She has dragged me from my books, whirled me downstairs, and locked me up in the back cellar. Screaming and kicking; but I've been over-powered. She stands in the place of a mother to me, she hisses, and so she has the right to inflict this punishment.

My prison is a whitewashed cube, lit by a tiny barred window high up in the far wall. I sit in the centre of it, wrists crossed behind my back, my arms and legs tied by strips of bandage to the heavy white chair, gilded and ornate, whose claw feet sink into the earth floor.

It hurts to breathe. Air like snow crystals scrapes my skin. I'm wearing only a petticoat; I'm barefoot; the cold, striking my goosepimpled flesh, turns it blue. My toes can't curl up and away because I'm trussed by the ankles. Once, the cold was only outside me. Fool: I stretched out my arms to clasp it. I stuck and burned. Like trying to embrace a block of ice. Now the cold has got inside me. Ice vapour wraps me in a shawl of frost.

How long since I last ate? Time is a blank white corridor. I ricochet down it banging against the walls; then back again. The gaps between meals are so long I'm stupid with hunger; can't even imagine any more what food tastes like. What is food? Something I'm not allowed to have.

Famished longing scours me out, sticks my belly against my spine. A thousand little knives, tips pointed and sharp, jab into my stomach, over and over again. Sometimes they catch, and twist, turning around in the bloodied slits they've made, wounds like little mouths screaming in harmony.

Occasionally the door at the top of the stairs opens, and Madame Heger appears, treads down with a tray, shovels a bowl of pap into me, departs. I'm not in control of this feeding; the spoon bangs at my teeth, dives into my mouth too far; I choke and dribble. I gobble at the food and I'm afraid I'll gag on it and I'll never swallow fast enough before it is withdrawn, leaving me still starving.

I imagine biting through the window glass, in order to shout for help, and my mouth filling with blood. I imagine biting off my hands and feet in order to free myself from the chair. I imagine gnawing at my own breast to feed myself, at my own entrails. Hurting myself enough so that I'll die and put an end to it.

But she doesn't want me dead quite yet. First of all she has a few lessons to teach me. Anger does not exist in her neat little house. So she pours hers into me; I belong outside; I'm her rubbish, to be chucked out; I'm her anger bucket. I pour all the anger in the house into myself. Learning self-control. That's what she wants me to learn. To be my own jailer. To punish myself whenever the system goes wrong. If ever I feel the start of warmth I shall rip off my fingernails or slash at my hair with wild scissors; I'll scratch the insides of my arms until I draw blood. If I can't get rid of anger altogether I'll give it just a tiny bit of house-room, at my edges: torn-off fingernails, torn-off toenails, chopped-off tufts of hair.

Good Charlotte.

Around the walls hang the naked bodies of women who weren't so good. Madame Heger points them out. Madame Bluebeard her real name is. Here they are, the bad girls, strung up by butcher's hooks stuck through the lips of their cunts. Their nipples. Their mouths. Madame Heger wears leather bracelets studded with curving hooks. She wears long false nails made of razorblades. When she lifts her claw and strokes you then you bleed. That's love, she tells me: sentimental little fool, stupid little idealist; you don't know that real love involves real pain. It must hurt or it's not love. She puts her arms around me and embraces me; I relax; she cuts me; then she croons and smiles and kisses it better again.

Sometimes she sits down opposite me in a second white chair. She hands me paper, pen and ink, and insists I write. My confession. What I've done and what I feel and what I fantasise. So that she can punish me again.

I sit there stolid as a potato greening in the dark. I'm so dull that she loses interest, gets up, leaves. The door clanks shut behind her.

It's better not to write. It's better to starve. It's better to wait here, hidden underground.

To pass the time away I recite the lessons you and she have taught me, *cher* Monsieur.

Cut off your hands so they can't want to touch him.

Cut off your feet so they can't want to run to him.

Cut off your lips so they can't want to kiss him.

Cut out your heart so it can't insist on loving him.

Peel off your skin. Roll it up, off, over your head; drop it. So you're untouchable. Reborn; blooming in blood. Unrecognisable as human.

That's the ghoul, Monsieur. Simply a woman in love. Searching for you; padding upstairs on her bloodied feet; blundering towards you over the tips of knives. Innocent and faithful as a dog; she runs to and fro in her tight, confined space, head down, shaking her grizzled mane; uttering sounds you can't translate. In the night she tries to come to you but she can't reach you. You're too well defended; your chamber door is locked and Madame Heger keeps the key. No chance that the madwoman can break in and bite, tear your flesh, sink her teeth into your neck. As you imagine, in your nightmare, she longs to do.

The woman who loved you was called Charlotte. She was clean and neat and had inky cuffs and was polite. She's not that monster you hear racketing to and fro, locked up in the cellar, rattling the lock and crying to be let out. Oh – poor monster. Take pity on her. You call out, start up in bed; your wife soothes you, and you lie down again and sleep.

But I, the nameless one; I prowl your house, your dreams; up and down, up and down; my mouth stuffed speechless with one of my own blank manuscripts.

PART TWELVE

The day after the party was a Sunday. Even though Sunday was now Adam's only time for writing, he began it with a lie-in, the luxury of long, uninterrupted sleep. Recently Robert had begun to crash about in his dreams and turn them into nightmares. But when Vinny slid in uninvited Adam smiled.

Language was the site of dreams. You discovered a new element. You lowered yourself down through the surface of life, lifting the lid on the street, your legs dangling above runny words; a different fluency; those rivers, like the Fleet, that flowed secretly underneath the city, from Hampstead Heath down through Kentish Town towards the Thames. Sleep opened the door to that other world, that fairy kingdom glimpsed like a reflection in a calm lake; the inverse of the day-to-day. Mountains turned upside-down, so that to climb was to dive and to fall was to fly.

When you were drifting towards sleep your boat took you through an archway cut in the rock, into a tunnel of water, and in this river leading underground the words of normal daily life broke free from their strings and casing and circled your heads like bats. Dreams flowed together, joining up your separate nights; you swam in them. Strange expressions formed on your tongue; you relished the salty peculiarity of words, how they wanted to shake loose and dance and form into phrases never heard before. New connections between words, new juxtapositions, half-lines of poetry: everything was happily crazy, topsy-turvy; it was fine; it was allowed; it was playtime.

Once Adam was fully asleep he had entered that country of larking about, puns, jokes, balderdash, gobbledegook, helter-skelter translations. Like a children's book, savage as *Struwwelpeter*, brightly illustrated with woodcut prints in primary colours, images aggressive as the serrated edges of sawn-open tin cans, fantasies cut into terrifying or erotic shapes. You were the emperor with powers of life and death; you were the enchanter turning enemies to stone. Refreshing, hurdy-gurdy stuff. But at the same time you were the unloved one hung upside-down and flayed alive; you were the traitor being disembowelled then burned; and you were the naked infant, starving and bawling, abandoned alone in the snow.

Waking up meant surfacing from that deep country, your treasures gleaned below clutched in your arms; you kicked out and rose towards the day, broke free of the green waters, fell on to land. Then you saw your trove differently, by day-light: pearls turned to chips off milk-bottle lips, diamonds to sparkles of grit shovelled along the gutter, emeralds to the heels of wine bottles; turned again, to litter dropped on the shore, rubbed smooth by the sea. You were a scavenger sort-ing through other people's rubbish, finding out what you considered beautiful: a length of green plastic tubing, drift-wood bent into odd shapes, bleached chunks of bones.

Vinny regularly scavenged along the Thames at low tide. Would you like to come with me next time? she asked, and he said yes. They walked east from Westminster, bent into the wind. He began telling her about the opening scene of *Our Mutual Friend*, the boat making its way down the Thames towards Tower Bridge, the terrified girl rowing her corpse-hunter father and their dreadful cargo, but Vinny interrupted him. Look at the sky. Pearly grey; high white trails of aeroplanes writing the names of drowned people. They climbed down on to the beach at Queenhythe. Vinny pointed. White tubular objects lodged in the sand. She bent down and picked them up, displaying them in her palm for Adam to see. Pieces of old clay pipes. Lengths of stem; fragments of bowl. She poured the creamy broken bits, clinking, into the deep pocket of his overcoat. She looked up at him. Olive-green eyes, the same colour as the river. Now her hand was full of something else she'd picked up. What was it? Show me, he begged. He kissed her. Her lips were soft and dry and tasted of salt.

A gull screamed in his ear and he flinched away from the sharp beak. No, not a gull. A factory whistle. A danger signal. Wake up, Adam. Adam, get up.

At some level, all night, he'd been aware of Catherine thrashing about, tossing off the covers, turning from side to side. Now, as the alarm beeped, he felt her roll away on her side of the bed, heard her yawn and sigh as she punched the button on top of the clock with unnecessary force. Gestures designed to prod him into waking. She wanted sympathy: she'd forgotten to turn off the alarm the night before. Sorry, Catherine, but that's your fault. He fisted the sheet and pulled it over his face. He registered her bad temper in the heaviness of her footsteps, her soft oaths as she rummaged for clothes. He rolled over into the warm space she'd left, sealed his eyes shut, and plummeted back into the darkness. But the dream had vanished and would not return. It had ebbed out like the river tide, leaving flotsam in its wake: a phrase or two; the image of a closed hand.

He pulled himself out of bed. Opened the curtains. Through the wreath of dripping clematis the sky was a marbly grey. The small green box of garden was dissolved to rain.

Something white hovered at the far end of the oblong of grass. Adam put his hands on the window-sill, leaned forward, stared through the streaming glass.

Robert. His father hunched silently in the rain, bare-headed, his shoulders streaming with wet, his arms dangling at his side. He looked patient and dogged, as though he'd been out there, waiting, all night.

Adam blinked. His father lifted a hand, waved, and vanished. White blossom jigged on the branches of the apple tree.

Adam jerked the curtains to and went into the bathroom. His hands were shaking, so that he shaved too fast and cut himself. Back in the bedroom, he rummaged in the chest of drawers for a clean T-shirt. None to be seen. He went to the pine cupboard in which hung all his father's clothes. Perhaps Catherine had made a mistake after doing the ironing and hurled all the clean linen in there. When he opened the door his father stared back at him. He was standing just inside, naked except for a pair of underpants.

Even as he slammed the door shut Adam registered that Catherine had cleared out all Robert's things. She hadn't consulted him. She'd just bundled up all the old man's clothes and got rid of them.

He put yesterday's T-shirt back on. He felt shuddering and sick. He told himself the nausea was just a hangover. It was not going to stop him getting down to work. Everything was going to be all right. It was only mid-morning. Ten or so. Plenty of time. He had the place to himself and three hours until lunchtime.

He lurched into the kitchen, rubbing his chin and yawning, to make coffee. The radio barked: a scratch of newsreader voices. Catherine was jabbing with the tip of the bread knife at a domed stain, crusted like a scar, on top of the cooker. From the doorway he watched her lunging gestures. Not delicate enough to be fencing. As though she were disembowelling an enemy. The dream stirred in him. He recognised the stain, a burnt black spread, lacy and crisp, as spilled melted cheese from last night's canapés.

– Hi, he said.

She turned her back and grunted.

Their agreement, now that the boys had gone away and

he'd taken up the carpentry job at the gallery, was that she wouldn't be around on Sunday mornings. He was left alone, which meant he didn't have to speak to anyone, could let his mind rest undisturbed, still in the world of the unconscious. Then the first line of a paragraph could come, floating easily into the calm space surrounding him. He was soothed by the emptiness of the house, could flow out and inhabit it while he slapped butter on to toast and tipped milk into coffee. He didn't have to have ego, edges. If he could begin Sunday properly, which meant by himself, in peace, then he could choose how to organise his work, how to use the time, discover exactly what he needed to do. With another person rattling about, obtruding their personality, his writing self shrank back inside its shell. Words killed stone dead.

– Why haven't you gone out? he said: what's wrong?

She picked up on his tone immediately. He saw her trying not to snap back. She raised her voice above the blare of news.

– I've been finishing the clearing-up from last night.

He walked over to the radio and turned the sound down.

– I'm going out in a minute, Catherine said: I thought I might go to Spitalfields market. But it doesn't get going much before eleven. I told you last night, before the party, I'd be leaving later than usual. Why can't you remember?

– Too much booze, he said: all your fault.

This ancient and feeble joke failed to pacify her. She glared at him. He gazed about, rubbing his nose, for the electric kettle. Someone had moved it, he could swear. Catherine flung knife and sponge in his direction. He dodged as they flew past him and landed in the sink.

She opened the fridge, got out some eggs, cracked them into a bowl, whisked them together. She laid two slices of bread under the grill.

– Not scrambled eggs again, Adam said.

– They're for me, Catherine said: I'll be out all day. Give you some peace and quiet. That arts festival on the South Bank is still on. I'll go to that after Spitalfields. If I'm not here this afternoon then you'll be able to get more writing done.

– You don't have to do that, Adam said: don't be such a martyr. It's your Sunday as well.

Catherine clattered the whisk on to the table, where it dribbled yellow. She fetched a saucepan from the cupboard and set it on the stove. She dug out a lump of butter from the butter-dish and scraped it into the pan.

– I'm not being a martyr. I'm just trying to help. And last night Charlie suggested I might like to drop into the gallery some time and have a look at it. See how things are coming along. I haven't been inside for ages.

Catherine poured the liquid eggs into the hot butter. She began to stir them with a wooden spoon.

– He won't be there on a Sunday, Adam said: he sees his daughter on Sundays.

– He's divorced? Catherine asked: I didn't know he'd been married.

– He'll want us to think about going over to France soon,

Adam said: check whether there are any paintings there we've forgotten about. Make some slides to show him.

Once the boys were in late teenage they had become bored with country holidays. Adam and Catherine had ceased taking them to visit Robert in the Sarthe so often. He'd stopped running his summer painting classes, and now he increasingly let out the house as a *gîte*. He emptied it of anything worth stealing, and locked up his few valuables, together with his paintings, away from visitors' prying eyes.

– Where have we put the key of the shed where he keeps everything? Adam asked: I suppose it's upstairs somewhere.

– I don't think we ever had it here, Catherine said: it must still be in France.

She spooned scrambled eggs on to toast.

– Why don't we ask Vinny to go over for us? she said: her residency's finished, she's planning to visit Jeanne in any case, she's bound to be broke. We could pay her to take some slides and do some clearing-up at the same time. If you're going to sell Les Deux Saintes, it'll need emptying.

– Poor little Vinny, Adam said: I didn't realise she was broke. She never lets on.

– Not so little as all that, Catherine said: she's fifty-two. And actually she's rather overweight.

Adam began to rummage on the dresser.

– Where do we keep aspirins? I've got a headache.

Catherine stood by the door, holding her plate of breakfast. She spoke in a light, controlled voice.

– By the way, the dishwasher's out of order. And we ought to wash this floor. It's absolutely filthy.

– We can do it tonight, for heaven's sake, Adam said: I've got a lot of work to do today.

– And then lavatory paper, Catherine said: we're nearly out of it.

– Calm down, Catherine. I'll go out and get some later, okay?

– Don't you tell me to calm down, she shouted: just take some responsibility for this bleeding household, that's all I ask.

– Fuck off, he shouted back.

She slammed her plate down on the table and stormed out. He swallowed some aspirin, discovered there was no coffee. They'd used it all up at the party. He made himself a pot of tea instead, and took it upstairs to his workroom.

He lit a cigarette and tried to think. He couldn't concentrate. Anger boiled inside him like hot oil. Useless. He could do nothing until it subsided. Nowadays, working for Charlie, he was always too tired in the evenings to do anything but slump in front of the TV. All he had were these few hours once a week. He must try not to be beaten by his bad mood. He stubbed out his cigarette, breathed deeply, swigged his tea.

The room scraped at him, its shapes and colours jarring. The wooden Noah's Ark on the side table, which he'd made for the boys when they were small, filled him with desolation. They hadn't emailed for two weeks. They had sailed off and perhaps were capsized; lost. Not so long ago they were giggly creatures with whom he could wrestle on the floor, babies whom he could pick up, one in each hand. You blinked, and they'd become taller than you, patting you fondly on the head before strapping on their ridiculous great rucksacks, snails lurching along under their domed houses, and departing on the New Age hippie trail. Perhaps they'd fall in love with India so much they'd never come back.

The window was a grey blank, a glass sheet of water like the side of an aquarium. As he glanced away from it, something white flicked past the corner of his vision, glimmered outside in the garden. He twitched the curtains shut. He picked up a book and tried to read. The words danced up and down. He willed himself not to open a crack in the curtains, not to look out of the window. Robert was not there. He'd been tidied up and thrown away by his daughter-in-law. How practical, how ruthless, Catherine could be. She had refused to have the plastic jar of Robert's ashes in the house. Put them on the garden if you want. Some days after the cremation, therefore, Adam had dug a hole in the rose-bed and emptied the ashes into it. Then he had put a mulch of compost on top, and a neat green turf like a lid.

His resentment went on hammering in his brain. Now Catherine was on the telephone in the hall. Her voice echoed up the stairs. Presumably complaining to one of her women friends. He felt her presence like sandpaper on his skin. She came at him through all these feet of separating air, pursuing him. Making sure he heard her feeling hurt, feeling

196

misunderstood. Tramping about downstairs, opening and shutting cupboards, letting doors bang, clacking across the tiled floor of the kitchen. The front door slammed. She'd gone out at last.

He unlocked the filing cabinet, took out the tumbler and the bottle of vodka, poured himself a stiff one. He sat back in his swivel chair, put his feet up on the edge of the open steel drawer. The vodka swept down his throat. It was like a caress. He poured another.

The inner tumult began to subside. Warm now, and blurry. The alcohol pushed the rage away to the other end of the room. At the same time it built a spike of resistance inside him. A knife sheathed in velvet. If anyone did come barging in now he would rise, seize them by the scruff of the neck, drop them out of the window. Offer them up to that white jiggery-pokery in the garden.

He suddenly wished that Vinny would ring him. Or simply arrive. Stand outside his castle walls and call up: can Adam come out to play? He wanted to go for a walk with her, somewhere in the centre of town, explore the deserted streets and alleys of the City, or stroll by the river, watching the way that the sharp wind whipped pink into her pale cheeks. Vinny didn't continually criticise him. She talked about other things than dishwashers and dirty floors. They could argue about writing, her absurd theories of the imagination as an inner, unconscious space versus his of a sort of moon rocket. The point of the imagination was that it let you get away from yourself. From your known self, Vinny said. It let you travel, Adam insisted. We're talking about the same journey in different words, Vinny said. Escape. As the boys were doing.

The vodka made his heart both warm and cold. Ever since the boys left home and went off on their trip, a month before Robert's death, Catherine had been moody and strange. Perhaps she minded that they hadn't offered to come back for the funeral. Perhaps she simply missed them. He did too, but he had more sense than to try to hold on to them, make them feel guilty for wanting to get away. He sensed that Catherine was discontented but in what way he didn't know. Rather than telling him what was the matter, she had started going on at him, trying to get him to do what she called opening up. She kept probing him, urging him to talk about his feelings. What he was feeling was depressed, but he suspected she didn't really want him to tell her about it. She just wanted to say the right, sensitive, womanly thing. To appear correct and loving. Tick for behaving well. Then she had the high moral ground yet again and he was just this pathetic male. Well, fuck her. He'd had enough.

He padded downstairs to the telephone, and called Vinny.

When she answered, there was an echo on the line. A roaring, rushing sound, as though they were under the sea.

– Are you free this afternoon? Adam asked: would you like to meet somewhere for a cup of tea?

Her voice came to him warmly and immediately, as though she were breathing very gently next to him, her lips brushing his ear.

198

– I can't today. I'm writing. It'll have to be tomorrow. After that I'll be gone.

– If you're planning to go to France, he said: would you be able to check the house for us? Take some photographs of Robert's pictures?

– Catherine already asked me, Vinny said: she rang me earlier this morning, and I said yes. She told me more about the show as well. I hadn't realised it could happen so soon. That's great news, Adam.

Back upstairs he took another shot of vodka and sighed. The pain was dulling, and his limbs were pleasantly weak. He stumbled across the room, kicked off his shoes, lay down on the sofa, banged his head on to the cushion and fell asleep. He dreamed he was a boy again, back in the house in France, watching Robert dance with a girl with a black hood over her head, slits cut in it for eyes. They polkaed out of the studio, into the garden. The girl seated herself on a swing hung over the wild long grass and Robert pushed her. She was plump and fresh as a little flirt by Fragonard. Kicking out her arched feet in beribboned high heels. Laughing. Her skirts flew up, blew backwards over her thighs, showing off her neat cunt.

The house was empty and fragile as a pierced and drained eggshell. He floated through it, his feet off the ground; he drifted up and down the stairs like wreathing mist. He knew he was dead. He was a ghost, at liberty to pass through walls, enter whatever rooms he chose, sleep in whatever bed took his fancy. Robert was a ghost too. They wandered together, looking for somewhere to lie down and rest.

When he awoke it was early afternoon. He felt very sick. He lurched into the bathroom and threw up. Then he showered and cleaned his teeth. He got himself downstairs, gulped a pint of water from the tap. He lay on the sofa in the sitting-room and watched an old film on television. At five o'clock he went into the kitchen to make a cup of tea. Catherine's plate of uneaten breakfast reproached him from the table. He shovelled the mess of eggs and toast into the bin. She'd left her laptop on top of a pile of papers, next to a clear perspex box of disks. He glanced at the label on the foremost one. *Angels in Corsets*. Presumably research notes for her Victorian literature class. *Middlemarch*, perhaps. Or something on women characters in Dickens. On impulse he sat down at the table, switched on the laptop, flicked through the box of disks. Odd titles. *Lessons in Restraint. The Discipline Exercise.* He ought to take more of an interest in Catherine's teaching. She acted as his unofficial editor, read and discussed everything he wrote. He ought to give more back. He selected a disk called *Beaten*, and began to read.

Just as he was finishing the washing-up he heard Catherine's key in the door. She came into the kitchen clutching a paper-wrapped cone of red and pink carnations and green ferns, a plastic bag bulky with shopping.

She jerked her chin towards the flowers held under her arm.

— For you. I got the papers as well.

She put her burdens down on the table. A roll of lavatory paper fell out of the carrier, a jar of instant coffee. She picked up the garish bouquet and held it out. He took it from her.

He loathed carnations. These were frilly as tutus. Cherry-red and sugar-pink; their green stems waxy as candied angelica. People wore them as cheap button-holes for weddings. He and Catherine had married in a register office, and he had forbidden flowers, all similar nonsense like confetti and tiered cakes. At the last minute he'd relented, and allowed her to accept the bunch of lily-of-the-valley that Vinny had run out to buy.

– I went to the garage on Holloway Road for the shopping, Catherine said: nowhere else was open.

He placed the flowers, still in their paper sheath, on top of the fridge. He gazed around.

– Where do we keep vases?

Catherine was looking at him. Wary. Checking for possible danger signs. Adam felt as though he were very ancient, made of stone, a stone man left outside all winter long, streaks of moss greening his shoulders, the rain beating against his back. A stone sentinel in a park, tall hedge of close-clipped yew at his back. He was scoured white by the weather. His nose was eroded, his fingertips, his toes. A stone man couldn't do what was required of husbands. Talk. Sort things out. He could only bend down and fill his mouth with earth. He wanted to go back to bed and sleep for ever.

Catherine seemed like a person in disguise. Was she really his wife? She had such a blank, polite face. She was a writer of sado-masochistic feminine crap. She was merely acting loving him. She opened her arms, walked forwards, hugged him. He put his arms around her, stiffly.

— Sorry I was so cross, she said.

She was clinging to him. He forced his lips to move.

— I'm sorry too. I was a bastard.

— It was me, Catherine said: I was being stupid.

He sighed. The lid was back on the box. He hadn't the energy to confront her with what he'd read. Let her keep her pathetic shitty secret.

— I rang Vinny too, he said: she told me you'd rung her. You shouldn't have asked her to go to the house before I'd said yes. Why couldn't you wait until I'd thought about it?

She tightened her grip. She laid her face against his shoulder.

— We seem to be going through such a horrible time. I just want us to be happy again. With Robert's show coming up, I want everything to be sorted out.

He patted her carefully, as though she might break. Perhaps she was stone too. A stone woman. Two toppling people of stone, propping each other up.

Catherine moved out of his embrace. She picked up the carnations, took a vase off the dresser, thrust the flowers into water.

— How was the festival? he asked.

— Good. I stayed to watch a bit of *Hamlet* done outside the National Theatre. Perhaps that effigy you saw was part of a rehearsal for Ophelia.

He hadn't told her Vinny had made the effigy, that he'd stood with her at Queenhythe and watched it drift away, wrenched free of the raft, further downstream, making for Greenwich and the open sea. He imagined Vinny wouldn't have mentioned it. Self-protection. Catherine had little time for playfulness. She had not a lot of patience for what she described as Vinny's nonsense. She didn't like to think of artists as having a necessary childish streak. All very well for them! Someone's got to earn the housekeeping, bring up the children, clean the place, cook the food. When she was teaching, he knew that she stressed to her students that making real, beautiful literature was very hard work. It certainly did not involve messing about as though you were still in the sandpit. What a hypocrite she was, writing that rubbish porn at the same time. He'd caught her on several occasions, tapping away in the kitchen, when he came in from work, and she'd jumped up, blushing. She'd never shown him anything. Now he knew why.

She brushed past him, holding the vase in both hands. He followed her into the sitting-room. He turned the television back on and threw himself down in front of it on the sofa. Catherine placed the vase of flowers on a mahogany side table, next to a Staffordshire shepherdess, a pile of books. He shifted his position, so that the carnations were out of view. He concentrated on the screen. He watched a game show. They ate supper in front of the television, seated together in silence. Catherine went to bed early. He sat on downstairs with a whisky. He listened to the house creak and grunt around him. As though it were grumbling under its breath, gathering its angry forces, determining to speak.

Adam found Monday a relief after Sunday. He'd always hated Sundays, the afternoons especially. Charlie was good to work for; let him do things in his own way, at his own speed.

At three o'clock he downed tools. He kicked off his boots and unbuttoned his blue cotton overalls, faded from washing, shrugged them off. He'd had them for twenty years. They were soft, from long wear, and creased. They concertinaed down. He stepped out of them, and they fell, wrinkling into twin flattened paper lanterns, on to the concrete floor.

– I'm off, he shouted up to Charlie.

Charlie's boots clattered down the stone stairs. Charlie's big hand pushed open the heavy double doors and he came in. He was carrying a metal tape. Dust on his toecaps, cobwebs in his hair.

– I've got to go over to the woodyard, Adam said: sort out that delivery.

The job had gone smoothly up until now. The warehouse roof had been patched up; the roofers had gone. Adam had separated off a space behind the main gallery, to make Charlie's office. Upstairs he had built walls of wooden screens, slatted in lengths of four by two, hung with nailed-up sheets of plasterboard, to make two good-sized studios that Charlie could rent out. Downstairs, where load-bearing and soundproofing were major issues, he had used breeze-block. The new spaces reminded him of the upstairs rooms in his father's house in France: the same dazzling white smoothness. Charlie's future office would double as a private showroom where he could talk to interested clients. Adam was going to build storage racks, fitted with sliding doors, for prints and drawings, and a big sweep of desk and display cabinets. The first batch of MDF he had ordered, ready for starting later that week, had not arrived. A good excuse for leaving.

Charlie was blowing his nose, wiping dust off his face with his handkerchief.

– Shall we have a quick drink later, talk about the show? Or are you off home after the woodyard?

– Another time, Adam said: maybe tomorrow.

He sat down on a packing-case and bent to pull his boots back on. He yanked them hard over his thick socks. Boots were no protection. His anger at Catherine felt too close to home. The ground under his feet, baked hard after a long draught, was suddenly cracking and breaking up. You thought you were in your own garden, neatly fenced in, safe, but now, inside your barriers, the earth sank away, collapsed. An enormous parched mouth opening to snatch at you. Don't fall into that trap. Speechlessness saved you. That way you did not betray weakness but stayed in control.

He donned his tweed jacket. Old and shapeless, it fell round him. He said goodbye to Charlie and departed.

From the woodyard behind Borough High Street he drove north. He left the car in the Safeway car-park off Holloway Road and walked back a couple of hundred yards, just past the railway bridge and the tube. He was due to meet Vinny in the Flora café, his favourite greasy spoon. This was where he used to eat lunchtime fry-ups sometimes in pre-Charlie days, when he was writing at home and needed to get out of the house.

He liked the Flora precisely because it wasn't fancy; wasn't owned by an American chain. If you wanted coffee it came hissing and spluttering out of an ancient machine; shot into your cup bitter and sludgy and black. To eat you could have an English breakfast, or breadcrumbed escalope with spaghetti, or tinned soup, or meat dish of the day with mash. The Flora catered for locals, who nodded hello, then put their heads down and ate; left each other alone. Carlo cooked and Bettina served. She shouted the customers' orders over the counter, and he shouted complaints back. Their duet rose and fell throughout the day; kitchen opera.

The café walls were fitted with tongue-and-groove, the brown paint flaking and shabby, up to dado level. Above was wallpaper, beginning to curl at its top edge. A lattice pattern in beige against a blue background, with the green leaves and curling tendrils of vines, spilling bunches of black grapes, twining in and out of the lattices. Here and there hung decorative 1950s soup-plates glazed dark blue, inset with circular photographs and edged with shells, from Italian seaside resorts. A window-sill bore a large cactus and a laminated Italian calendar showing St Peter's. A phosphorescent statue of the Virgin was tucked in beside the till. The radio buzzed and chattered in a corner. Carlo's big black frying-pan sputtered and spat. He was cooking strips of bacon, flipping the rashers over as they crinkled up and the rinds hardened from translucent to gold.

It was raining outside, and the café was stuffy, two fan heaters blasting out scorched air. Smell of damp coats and perspiration as well as of crisping fat. Adam and Vinny sat at a table near the door, cups of tea in front of them on the blue and white checked plastic cloth. The nearby window was steamed up. Vinny drew on the wet glass with her forefinger. A glum face, mouth turned down.

– That's you, she said: what's up? Are you thinking about Robert?

Adam moved his shoulders inside his jacket. The thick tweed constricted him. He was much too hot. He took the jacket off and hung it over the back of his brown wooden chair.

– Tell me about your day first, he said: what have you been doing?

– Writing, Vinny said: the usual. I was finishing something so that later this afternoon I can get on with my packing. I've booked the ferry for France for tomorrow. No point hanging about.

– You know we're thinking of selling Les Deux Saintes, Adam said: once we've sorted out the pictures. We'll need to start emptying the place. It'll be in a real mess, Vinny. There's a lot of clutter.

– Are you sure you're not rushing it, Vinny asked: selling the house so soon after Robert's death? Shouldn't you wait a bit?

She hesitated.

– You must have a lot of childhood memories associated with that house. Won't it make you sad to get rid of it so quickly?

Adam grimaced at her. Questions questions questions. There she sat, downy and expectant as a baby bird, all mouth, beak open, squawking. His duty, apparently, to fill her up with ribbed red-purple worms.

Her words had jabbed him in the stomach. She wasn't soft and babylike at all. She had talons. With that beak of hers she was tearing him open. Poking his insides apart, pecking up pieces of gut. Just like children do. He used to collect up dead sparrow fledglings fallen from nests in the high gutter, give them funerals, bury them in the garden with crosses made from lollipop sticks. Then afterwards he dug them up and did post-mortems with a spent match, a penknife. Irresistible, the need to prod those thin, flopping necks, those skin-sac bellies, distended and greyish-pink. No feathers. They were hardly birds at all, which was what gave you permission to slit them apart. Bloody blackish goo. Disgust meant they were well dead, so kick them on to the metal coal shovel and tip them into the dustbin.

– How long have I got? he asked: fifty minutes, isn't it, the analytical hour?

Vinny looked taken aback.

– I didn't mean to offend you.

She was pink in the face. Nevertheless she returned to the attack.

– Why is it if I ask you a personal question you think I'm prying? I've known you for twenty-seven years but you never speak about your childhood at all.

– Well, Adam said: it's all made up, memory, isn't it? That's the current wisdom, isn't it? But if you really want to know, my memories of childhood are not brilliant. So I shan't mind selling the house and getting rid of them. Not at all.

Adam didn't have anyone he could tell. Not as a child and not later on. He didn't know that you could tell. Everything was private and nobody interfered. People punished children. Boys got hit all the time; it was normal. Adam admired the bad boys at primary school who tried to get away with as much mischief as they could, even when they knew they faced a walloping. He wasn't brave enough.

He went to the pantomime once with his parents. *Peter Pan.* You could tell immediately who the villain was, not just from the roll of drums announcing his entrance, but from his glittering eyes and elaborate black wig, his thin mouth under twirly black moustaches, and of course from the evil hook at the end of his arm. Whereas Robert was big and curly-haired and smiled a lot. He liked going to the races and the cinema, drinking, and being out with his friends. Experimenting in his paintings should have been enough: stretching women's bodies into impossible postures, bending back their arms and legs like hairpins, corkscrewing their necks. That was art, its subject-matter not to be criticised. But he needed to twist real people about as well.

Outside the house Adam's parents were giants, tall as

electricity pylons piercing the sky. Heads haloed in aeroplanes they reared up above you, lover of gravity, where you stumbled and tottered then collapsed in the grass. They shot out their steel arms, collected fierce energy from the thundery clouds, and directed it downwards. In their metal hands they clutched wire bouquets that crackled and snarled. They strode the land and might trample you underfoot if you stood up and came too close. Better not try to look into their faces. Their gaze was terrible, could turn you to stone; strike you blind.

Parents were also dangerous back indoors because you could not be sure whether their power was turned on or off. If you put your fingers to the socket you might get a shock that would bounce you upside-down across the room; might stun you and lay you out for dead. In their hands you might be held, safe, but you might be dropped. It depended. You did not control the switch. Other people pressed it up or down. Your father might press your mother's switch and then stand back to watch her light up and glow, or flash into a glare and then explode.

When the bough breaks the cradle will fall down will come baby cradle and all.

The song sneaked into his head and sang itself without his wanting it, whether he was driving across town to Borough or talking to Charlie about shelf measurements or waiting to be served in the pub. The drop was always there, just beyond his feet, and the whirlwind might whip out at any moment to coil round the cradle, snatch the baby out, and toss it contemptuously into the abyss.

210

Sometimes his mother was not an electricity pylon but a shy animal. A fox who hid in the undergrowth and could not be coaxed out. He tracked his mother on Sunday afternoons, in the calm space after tea and before supper. His father dozing, the room comfortably dim, curtains drawn, firelight and warmth. Adam could creep up on his mother then, hover in her shadow. Watch her withdraw into her own place. She touched her china collection and went to earth.

She stooped, knelt in front of the cabinet, which looked like the building in that picture Robert had once shown him. It squatted, sturdy and pinnacled, in the corner of the sitting-room. In the picture the front had swung open like a dolls'-house door so that you could see in. Slice of interior sharp with dangly points, like a church. A white-faced girl with upraised hands, kneeling at a desk, looking scared, a winged man in a gold frock throwing flaming darts at her and burning up at the same time, a cat jumping away bristling and screeching. Topped with a carved roof like a bit of picture-frame. Adam's mother looked as though she were praying. Then she sighed, twisted the gilt key, pulled open the glass door.

Inside the cupboard lived her troop of little saints whom she loved, the figurines that glanced coolly back when you stared at them Monday to Saturday. They were all called donttouch. But they allowed his mother to approach on Sunday afternoons with Adam hovering at her side.

She took them out reverently, one by one; she caressed them with a yellow duster; she dipped the tip of a damp muslin cloth around the backs of their necks, behind their ears. Her good children who did not scream or kick or wet their beds. They did not grizzle or bite when thwarted. The little gods had smooth faces, tearless and unflushed. They were delicate; porcelain flesh, porcelain bones; needed constant nursing and attention. His mother's hands cupped them protectively. Their paleness gleamed against the dark mahogany of the cupboard doors.

They were all his mother's favourites. Girls and boys both. Some of the boys wore hunting dress, carried whips and horns, dogs frothing at their booted feet. They posed on silvery rocks frilled with tiny coloured flowers. The girls strode in pleated tunics and matched arrows to stretched bows. They tiptoed on green mounds and aimed at invisible prey. One of the boy figurines was content just to watch the others. He was like an older brother who'd never hit or tease you. He was sweet-faced, dreamy-looking, wearing a blue jacket, a big lacy collar, and long black trousers. The forefinger of his left hand was tip-tilted to his chin. Legs crossed at the ankle, he leaned against a stumpy white column, glancing at the open book balanced there. His hair curled; his hat was flung down beside him. In his left hand he carried a quill pen. Under his feet was a notice with his name on: Shelley. A girl's name. That was why his mother loved him so much. Adam's mother smoothed the invisible dust from his shoulders, stroked him all over.

Adam pointed to the china cabinet.

– Can I have him?

– No, darling, said his mother: they're not for children. They're not toys.

His mother mooned and dreamed. Hummed to herself; doting on her figurines; hidden inside a cocoon of porcelain. Adam waited until she'd left the room to answer the telephone in the hall, leaving the door of the cabinet open. Then he plucked up those china children one by one by the feet and smashed their heads against the savage edge of the cabinet to fly apart. The gut pleasure and relief of that crack, shatter, splintery mess: he too was a giant and he too could explode.

For one glorious moment he wasn't sorry. Haloed in freedom. He'd done exactly what he needed to.

Then his father woke up and roared. His mother ran back in, white-faced. How could you? How could you? His father hit him and she wept.

He was a spoilt child, they recognised. He'd been their darling, their one and only. Now they sent him away to school; for his spoiled parts to be mended and rubbed smooth. More like punishment, though. That was the story repeated in the prayers in the school chapel: of the fall; the punishment. Man who had danced with the angels now fell, toppled from the topmost rafter bracing the dark heights above the altar; that tower of sky; man stepped out into nothingness, fell, flew spiralling down the coil of air that collapsed and could not hold him up. Man's thin skin split; spill of his guts: he was splattered broken-necked like fledgling mess on the cold floor. The nave roof arched above Adam, built of angels jammed together with gold nails. He gazed up at it from the cramped pew, sweating and dizzy.

If you turned the whole place upside-down you could not fall. You could not get lost. The chapel, topsy-turvy, became Noah's boat. He drew pictures of it in scripture lessons, working out, precisely as possible, the tiered arrangement for the animals above and below decks, where to put the cabins for the people. He coated his parents in gold before taking them on board, sealed them carefully into a tiny cupboard in the fo'c'sle. The statue of his mother was the bigger one. She held her boy, swimming towards her in the sea of her lap, in the crook of her arm, kept them both steady as the gale rocked; she was white-faced because she was seasick. The ark was solidly built; watertight; tilting up and over precipitous waves; his mother did not fall off and she did not break.

The pictures unreeled, sharp and rapid and gaudy as cartoon films, in his mind; crayon in fist, he couldn't scrawl them fast enough. Later on he began to write short stories, experiment with sketching one frame at a time.

Now all he wanted to do was dovetail words together. He dropped out of university in his second year. He worked at labouring jobs while he wrote his first novel. Meanwhile his mother left home and his father got a divorce. He qualified for one more year of grant; took a carpentry course then wrote his second novel. Now he was launched. Art was safely impersonal; held away from himself; separate. Childhood was private; his secret thoughts; remained sealed away in the cupboard. You wouldn't dream of writing about it. Only blabbering confessional amateurs did that. The doors were firmly shut; no more breakages could occur; you got on with things.

He yawned. He felt a thick layer of the past lift off his back. Like a wing? Like a muffling coat? To be discarded. Then picked up and looked at. Tight knot of forgotten stuff packed small as a pea, teased out in his hands to become exuberant loops flying and tangling all over the place, then hauled back in like ropes, wound into a skein, woven into a story. He'd done it, like the girl in the fairy tale, weaving coats out of nettles for her brothers, the children of Lir, to cover their wings, to save them before she was burnt to death at the stake, to turn them from swans back into men again. Only she hadn't finished in time and so one brother had had to keep his single wing. Half swan, half man. Limping. Calling.

Vinny listened distractedly, fiddling her forefinger against the side of her thumb. While he talked, Adam had avoided her eyes, concentrated on the yellow plastic mustard bottle, the brown sauce bottle, the red ketchup bottle. He enjoyed the gaiety of their colours against the blue and white squares on which they stood. Bright as Noah's Ark figures bobbing across the sea. He longed for a cigarette. He wondered if Vinny had any on her. She didn't seem to be carrying a bag. She was wearing an oversized black sweater reaching to her knees, a skirt like a ballerina's *Sylphides* frock, its stiff layers of gauzy grey net dotted with brilliants, and black leather biker boots. Her black leather jacket was slung over the back of her chair.

She was gazing at him affectionately because he'd let her come close. Women liked that. As though they'd won in some sympathy contest. He had to struggle against feeling, in these moments, that they were out to get him, seize his fragile skull between their hands, smash his head against the wall. He knew that really it was the other way round. To protect her he had to hold Vinny off; behind invisible barbed wire. The impulses to violence, to hurting and destroying, must never be told. These you carried stoically inside yourself. The slashing and burning scarred only you. The people you were fond of remained safe, on the other side of your battle-thickened skin. The pain of those attacks inside made you grimace but no-one else need know.

Vinny reached out her finger and replaced the downturned mouth of her doodle on the glass with a smiling one.

– What's so amusing?

He remembered he'd been looking at her clothes.

– I like your outfit. Takes me back to the seventies.

Girls wearing crazy clothes had thronged the literature festivals. All kinds of performers, dressed up in carnival colours and costumes and chiffons. Sometimes there was one big venue; a circus-style tent or a church hall; sometimes you did the pub circuit. Rock music and stand-up comedy and poetry. The novelists had read out chapters of their novels like poems: Adam had sung his work, declaimed it, recited it like parts in a play. Mime artists, trapeze artists, dancers, singers, writers: they'd all shared stages, rowed and fought, got drunk, gone to bed together. The procession of ardent, sexy, passionate girls had tied it all together with gold ribbons. How generous, how easy, those girls were; those Pill-jugglers; how quick to signal their desire and claim their freedom; off with their boots and flounces, naked bodies laid against yours in a trice; so eager to suck your cock, try anal sex, prove themselves willing; up for anything. They fucked in the woods at music festivals, in the long grass on Hampstead Heath, on kitchen tables in squats, in each other's rumpled beds. Too many of them ever to remember all their names. Except Vinny, of course. And Catherine.

– Tell me more about your mother, Vinny said: you never have.

Adam frowned at her.

– What's there to tell?

She'd rejected him. She sent him away to school. Then she ran away herself. A wound too deep to be forgivable. He packed it with ice. He had built walls around himself to keep the hatred out. Then it was all over; done and dealt with. He could grow up and get on with his life.

Catherine had rescued him from his childhood by respecting his need for distance. She sat cross-legged outside his tower and waved. Had she locked him in and hidden the key? At certain moments hatred would suddenly rise up, shrieking, clattering its wings, like a swan disturbed by a gunshot. Then he had to break free and get out.

Catherine would certainly not want him to be roaming about, meeting Vinny in cafés on the quiet, talking intimately. Going to exhibitions with her sister was one thing; telling her his secrets was another. Sometimes Catherine was the gamekeeper, stalking him; keeping him within bounds. He told himself that was unfair. But he enjoyed talking to Vinny, despite her probing; in some moods he relished her naïveté, her idealism. She believed that being a writer meant following a vocation. Therefore she had opted not to lead a conventional life. If you did, she'd told him once, laughing, well, that was merely a disguise to keep your enemies off your back while you got on with what truly mattered. Er, like Philip Larkin. Adam had listened to her simplicities and smiled.

– You got a cigarette? he asked.

– I thought you were giving up, Vinny said.

– Can't talk about my fucking childhood without a cigarette, Adam said.

They were drinking tea. Cooling to the yellowy colour of clay puddles. He ought to be making a move. He ought to go to Safeway's and do the shopping, take it home, fly back to his wife on his single, unwieldy wing. Hovering on the pavement outside the café he would be transformed, from swan back into man. He would become Catherine's husband once more. Faithful as a swan to his mate. He had been faithful to Catherine throughout their marriage. Surely, he said to her in his head: that means something? But those sado-masochistic fantasies she'd been writing were a form of unfaithfulness. That kind of sex, those kind of games, disgusted him. She'd been betraying him, over and over, all these years.

He seized the words running inside his head and strangled them. Fool to have come out without cigarettes.

The warmth inside the café made him reluctant to go back into the wet, windy street. The warmth he felt from Vinny. With her he stopped being the stone man he'd been with Catherine all weekend. Vinny breathed life into him, turned him back to flesh and blood. But despite that he couldn't talk to her any more about his parents.

– I've got writer's block, he said: I'm done for. I can't write a word. I'm too depressed. I'm finished as a writer. That's why I took on the building job. Nothing to do with research. I just had to have something else to do. I haven't written a word for six months.

Then he was on his feet, the bill paid, ushering Vinny out, blinking at the downpour, putting up his umbrella. Crack and twang of the grey fabric as it snapped up, tautened, blocked off the rain. Of course Vinny didn't carry a brolly. She was shrugging herself into her leather jacket and grumbling at him not to rush.

They paused on the pavement outside the café. She caught his arm. Forced him not to start walking away. So he had to remember what he had just said. He had told no-one, certainly not Catherine.

Fatigue dropped on to him like a coat of nettles falling from the sky, half stifling him. He wanted to lie down on the pavement, cheek flat in a puddle, and drown in sleep. Traffic splashed past. He ordered his legs to begin moving. He pulled Vinny along.

After some moments Vinny halted their progress. She stood stock still in the middle of the pavement, so that pedestrians behind cannoned into her, had to dart round her, exclaiming and muttering.

– You need a muse. You haven't got one at the moment, have you? I can tell. That's your problem. It's simple.

He put his free arm around her and laughed aloud.

– Vinny, you're hopeless. What a romantic and old-fashioned idea.

Green eyes swivelled and regarded him.

– I love you, Vinny said: I wish I could help you.

She did not appear to require a reply. She stuck her hands in her pockets and stared at him.

– I never did stop loving you, she said: all these years. I thought I could handle it. It was just part of my life. And then at your party on Saturday it suddenly all burst up again, like a fountain being switched on.

Adam felt like a man in a cartoon, clutching his brow in exasperation and trying not to shout. Or else he was the man in that Blake engraving, arm flung up, clenched fist, drowning. Waves of emotion slopping over his head.

– Don't be so absurd, he said: you don't know what you're saying. I never heard anything so ridiculous.

He began to march them along the pavement towards Vinny's bus-stop. She'd refused a lift earlier. He held the umbrella with his right hand, his arm bent up, held in close to his side. Vinny, matching her pace to his, tucked her hand under his elbow. The umbrella arched over them, a grey satiny dome.

Adam felt he ought to make some gesture of conciliation.

Calm her down. She hadn't changed. She was as unpredictable and volatile as a child. He searched for neutral words. It was like tearing up a rotten draft and beginning a new one.

– You're so sweet, he said: what can I say? Thank you.

They tramped along to the pedestrian crossing, darted across in front of the impatient traffic, gained the pavement opposite. The familiar shopfronts flicked by, panels of doors and windows slick with wet. Here at last was the bus-stop coming up.

– It's not a very good idea, that's all, Adam said: is it? It's not wise. We're brother and sister, we're friends, and that delights me. I think we should keep it that way.

They stopped walking, entered the canopy of the bus-shelter. It was empty except for them. The street noise receded. They were held in a translucent cocoon, a bubble blown inside brimming wet, glassed in on three sides. Adam thumbed the catch on his umbrella, pulled at the metal bracelet stuck with thin ribs, drew down the dark skirts gleaming with raindrops. He shook out their frilled fullness, bunched up the damp pleats in the fingers of one hand and gripped the handle with the other, began to furl their silky smoothness, twisting the overlapping layers round and round. His right hand sought for the short strip of dangling ribbon, the little button on the end of it that was the catch.

Vinny was standing too close to him. He could smell her skin and her hair. Vanilla. Oranges. He put his arms around her, one hand still clasping the umbrella, and she put her arms around him. The umbrella, unfastened, loosened itself, flared out like a great poppy, a balloon of grey silk.

The 43 bus churned up to the kerb, spraying their feet and ankles with muddy water. He released Vinny and kissed her cheek. He searched for the words he hadn't been able to say twenty-seven years ago.

– I'm so sorry, Vinny.

She jumped on to the platform, grasping the metal pole in one hand to pull herself aboard.

– Ask Catherine who the model was for that painting in your bedroom, she cried: why don't you? Or is that something else you don't want to know?

Without looking back she clumped up the stairs to the top deck. He saw her gauzy grey skirt vanish; her black boots.

Vinny was shaking. She scrambled towards her favourite seat in the front, by the driver's periscope, just as the bus pulled away. They swerved and jolted, joining the main stream of traffic, and she nearly fell over. She dropped on to her seat, trembling. You couldn't smoke on buses any more. She'd made a heroic effort in the café and not smoked, because Adam was trying to give up. At the party he'd leaned away from her cigarette, frowning.

Now the nicotine withdrawal was really hitting her. Her insides were clamouring for a joint, or at least a cigarette. Above all, for the moment of sharpness and clarity that inhaling brought. A knife to the brain. Edges to yourself; less of the blurriness that came from talking to others, when you cracked open like eggs and let your wet yellow hearts flop out, break and leak into the whites, pool in the space between you. Once out, runny and transparent, how did you know you'd ever get yourself back in?

Her face felt thickened to crimson with blushing. What a fool she'd been. Behaving like a schoolgirl with a crush. How could she have been so stupid? No self-control. A middle-aged woman making an absurd spectacle of herself. Pathetic and grotesque. She'd embarrassed him. Disgusted him. She'd never be able to look him in the face again. She had betrayed her sister, as well. He loved Catherine. Of course he did. She ought to stand by Catherine and stick up for her at all times. She should have kept her secret. What could she have been thinking of?

She knew the answer to that one. Revenge. How horrible she was. What a bitch. What a cow. She wanted to crawl under a stone and die. She curled her fingers into fists, so that her nails attacked her palms.

Her empty mouth yearned for that slim paper tube of tobacco. Something safe to hold on to, that kept you anchored in the world and less liable to fly off; an umbilical cord; food of a sort; also a barrier between you and the other, a soft wall of smoke you could peer through, sometimes climb over. Hide behind. The bus was tilting along so fast she felt she might fall out of the wide window just in front. She clasped the steel rail with both hands and tried to breathe deeply. It was no good. Tears rose up, warm, spilled over. She invoked that sliver of ice Graham Greene said every writer had at heart, that chip of ice warning her she'd have to stop weeping in five minutes when the bus arrived at her stop. So have a nice cry in the meantime, said the chip of ice. But the ice floes were melting. They'd grind her to death. She'd fallen overboard. She was the monster thrown out of the Ark. The Flood overwhelmed her. She began to cry.

Part Thirteen

During this pause in my wanderings I continue to think of you, *cher* Monsieur. I burn my letters to you, as usual. Here, at Nohant, I give them to the housemaid to use as kindling. A fire in my bedroom – what luxury. I used to say I did not care for luxuries, but that, I realise now, was because I had none; whereas this château is full of them.

I'm writing this upstairs after dinner. The main bedrooms are all up here on the first floor, arranged, off corridors, in interconnecting sequences. For the first few days, I kept getting lost in what seemed a maze, and throwing open sets of double doors in the wrong direction. My windows look out over the flower garden at the side of the house. My hostess, Madame Sand, wants me to have all the quiet I need. She herself rises at dawn every day to write. Oh, she says, with a wave of the hand: just my little annual novel. I get up later than she does. I loiter under soft quilts in a neat four-poster, hung with pink and cream chintz, surveying my writing-table in cherrywood, the two little armchairs, and the cupboard carved with garlands of oak leaves and corn wreaths. My room is enormous, to one used to the parsonage at Haworth.

All the floors up here are of highly polished parquet; I hear the maid's heels tapping along the corridor from a long way off. The servants have their own little staircase, which rises in the middle of the house, easy of access from the kitchen quarters. The cook has her bedroom tucked away in a turn of those stairs. Madame Sand sympathises with the hardships of the local peasants' lives. She believes in the rights and dignity of the working man. But her family's château was not constructed to accommodate these beliefs. The maids live in cramped, unheated quarters overhead. Up and down they clatter in the morning, up and down, fetching hot water, and materials for lighting a fire, and a cup of hot chocolate if that's what you require; tending to all one's needs all day long.

You didn't know I was in France, did you? I don't think I wrote down the story of my journey to Paris. I was in an odd state during that time; not in the mood for writing. But now I'm settled here for the moment the old urge to write to you once more comes over me. Whatever happens to me, snatch of amusing conversation overheard or bizarre incident experienced or small adventure undertaken, you're still the one I want to tell about it. I hold back, of course, for fear of exasperating and boring you. Unlike Madame Sand, who has male friends, correspondents, confidants as a matter of course. She is the veteran of many love affairs, and that has made her confident.

Madame Sand does not look like a romantic heroine. Not in the least. Not until she glances up and shows you her big black eyes, which are still the eyes of a young woman, ardent and fearless. On the surface she seems placid, and serene. Wrinkles and grey hairs, a troop of visitors, children and grandchildren to keep her busy, an elevated position in her community, all her myriad love affairs well behind her. So she says. Calm and chaste in her lace cap, never to be suspected of passionate yearnings, eagerness for sex. She's over sixty; at first glance merely a cosy sibyl.

A lovely disguise: lady wolf dressed up as virtuous chatelaine. That's how you could do it, I see. Squat a gingerbread château in the woods; lure in the boys with offers of sugarplums. Lull them. Watch, bright-eyed, from your rocking-chair. Then what? She wants to gobble them up, smacking her lips over every delicious bit, but she knows she mustn't. If she pounces they'll flee, screaming, to fetch help, and then their fathers and brothers will come and burn her house down, flay her alive, make slippers out of her furry grey skin. Poor Mrs Wolf: she doesn't deserve to die. She just wants a lover or two. She behaves herself, Mrs Wolf, just as she ought. She controls herself. Instead of springing on people she writes novels. She lies in bed in her frilled nightcap and she makes up stories.

Do I believe her, that her love life is over? No. But she's a novelist, and telling lies is required of her. She gives me, for example, different versions of her past. Sometimes she's had thirty lovers. Sometimes forty. Sometimes so many that she can't remember the precise number, and certainly not their names. She has desired men and women both. The heart, she says, does not discriminate.

Her grandchildren clamour for her stories, just as I do. In the evenings, before they go to bed, she reads to them from the illustrated volume of Perrault, embroidering a bit, adding a few extra gothic touches, a few extra bloodthirsty details. My return to health is marked by my new-found relish of bright images, my reawoken pleasure in others' word-spinning. I'm hardly a convalescent at all any more.

Did I tell you that I'd been ill? Probably not. I forget. I was delirious, I do remember the doctor telling me that. He said I rambled; I cried out distressing things; I didn't want to see Arthur; I turned my face away even from Papa. Too much imagination; that's what the doctor said. His diagnosis was that I was ill in my mind: I'd gone away from those who loved me into a fairy world; I'd turned my back on real life for the sake of living in a story that was not my own.

Such a rousing story it was. You were in it, Monsieur. We floated through your walled garden in the sunlight; the grass was radiant, like green fire; arm in arm we sauntered down the gravelled *allées* between the flowerbeds to the central *berceau* crowned with leaping flames; and then we went further; over green hills, into the woods; and here we lay down in a glade of chestnut trees. You spread your coat for me; smooth wool hot with sun.

Every afternoon this story repeated itself. Oh, we were far from Haworth, I can tell you. Nor did we seem to be in Brussels: that city with its tight, confining rules. Instead we'd arrived somewhere in France, which made me laugh because in my younger days I'd been so suspicious of the French and their penchant for pleasure, and here we were learning to be like them. You were no longer a respectable Belgian professor: your *bonnet-grec* and *paletot* were abandoned, your spectacles flung down. I begged the doctor not to take me away, but he hauled me back to Haworth. Now, Charlotte, for the sake of your husband and father, you must try; you must make an effort to get better. I obeyed. Then, as soon as I was well enough, I packed a bag, took the train for London, and bought a ticket on the Channel packet.

In Paris I necessarily abandoned all my old shyness. Since I'd long been an admirer of Madame Sand's novels, I enquired for her address, then boldly went and called upon her. She invited me to come and visit her in the country. So here I am.

I've come back to reality. Which is the world of the imagination. That's the true world, Monsieur. Why did I ever allow myself to forget? You have to conjure it, that's all. Sometimes you can completely forget it's there. You get ground down in the minutiae of daily life, the details. And then it's as though a door swings open, a door concealed in the wall, and you walk through, and you're in that other place.

Night after night I dream I still live in Haworth, in our tiny, crowded house surrounded by tall looming tombstones. You've vanished to a far-off foreign land. I'll never see you again. Loss saws my insides. This is my life now, to the end of my days. Having to live without you, hold this wrenching absence, survive this pain.

Then I suddenly discover the parsonage is much bigger

231

than I thought. I find a door, in the back wall, which leads into another room; a secret one; and I go into it, and you're there. Waiting for me in that new place. You're not gone away after all; you're not lost; you exist, smiling, in flesh and blood; I find you; I can touch you.

These dreams weave through my enjoyment of the company of Madame Sand. We talk to each other for hours; sitting by the fire, or working in the garden, or over supper; about whatever we want. These conversations are nourishment for which I've been starving without knowing it; I eat them; I drink them in. She fills me up with good things. Talking to her, I'm reminded of my games with Emily, how we used to come home from walks on the moors and show each other the treasures we'd picked up; a feather; a sprig of heather; a round pebble from the brook; swap them from hand to hand. We'd arrange them on the window-sill; little shifting exhibitions of whatever had taken our fancy that day. With Madame Sand it's the same; we put a shape on things. Her mind is honest and inventive, springy and robust. She eagerly catches whatever words I want to throw at her, spins them in the air, tosses back her own.

I dreamed of you last night and so I awoke happy, here in my bedroom at Nohant. The sun shining on the polished wooden floor. The two worlds of night and day connected by that door swinging wide then beginning to close. You faded away behind me as I groped back towards the light of morning but I was able to leave you without too much sorrow. I knew you existed there in the darkness of the other world, waiting for me. You hadn't vanished for ever just because for the moment I couldn't see you. That's what the abandoned baby thinks, that her mother will never come back. The end of the world. She rages and weeps. That's what I was like when I was young; when I lost Emily; when I lost my own baby; when I lost you. But now I'm older, and I'm learning about true love; how indestructible it is.

So I clambered towards waking. The sun broke through the gap between the shutters, a white slash of light on the dark wooden floor, bright and imperious, ordering me to get up now. The maid came in, smiling, threw open the shutters and pronounced it a fine morning, emptied my wastepaper basket of crumpled up pages of letters, lit me a fire. I watched my words to you flare up then fall.

I was the first in the household down to breakfast. I took my cup of coffee outside, stood at the top of the steep flight of steps that leads down from the front door, and looked out.

So unlike the black stone and gloom and oppression of Haworth. Here there seems to be more light, sun, sky. The château, grey and compact, is set on one side of this small village, and is surrounded by tall trees. Lacy green foliage in every direction. The church bells bang out their iron song. Cocks crow. From beyond the stone walls surrounding us comes the lowing of cattle, the cooing of pigeons and doves, the barking of dogs, the cries of children, the singing and calling of people at work. When the Angelus rings, morning and evening, you hear them down tools and shout out a prayer.

I descended to the gravelled forecourt, and thence to the sanded paths of the flower-garden, to pick a nosegay for the breakfast table. Dew glittered on leaves and petals. Threads of mist, like the finest wisps of white wool, filled the hollows of the meadow beyond the low garden wall. As though sheep drifted past and their fleece caught on the fence. Though it was still early, and the air was cool, it was sweet as plums. Low, slanting sun furred the ground with gold. I chose a few white roses, some rusty pink chrysanthemums, some tawny dahlias, one or two blossoms from the sprawl of pale yellow climbing nasturtiums fallen in the long grass around a post. We ate breakfast outside, the pot of flowers next to the basket of rolls.

Later I worked in the vegetable plot with Madame Sand and her gardener Thomas. We harvested a basketful of green beans, several pumpkins, spinach that squeaked and jumped about in Thomas's hands as he crammed it into a sack to take back to the house. He talks with a strong local accent, using so many dialect words it is hard to understand him. He has a carved brown face; a face you see everywhere on the men here; merry and alive. He's teaching me his names for things. He handed me a bunch of long pods speckled pink and red. Are these beans? I asked. *Grelots*, he said: that's what we call them, they've got lots of names, we baptise them. Later, having shelled them, the cook baptised them; she practised total immersion; she boiled them for fifteen minutes precisely; and then we ate them, bathed in hot cream, for supper.

In the middle of the afternoon two old countrywomen

arrived, bringing gifts: bunches of blue asters tied with twine, a bowl of eggs, bouquets of parsley, big bags of walnuts. To say thank you to Madame Sand for curing their illnesses. Kill or cure, I'd have thought: she doctors them, poor wretches, with all kinds of infusions of herbs, which she stirs up in a little saucepan on the kitchen stove. Disgusting, weedy messes, bitterly sour-smelling, they are too. I've watched her concoct them. She is curing me too, but not with herbs, I'm glad to say.

And so goodnight, dear friend.

Charlotte

PART FOURTEEN

Catherine constructed her week to unroll, like a speeded-up film, in a blur of busyness. Work eat bed sleep work eat bed sleep. She was a tiny mannequin with jerking arms and legs, mouth open silently screeching. Any gaps in her frantic timetable she stuffed with shopping, cooking, washing, cleaning. Adam was distant, shut away behind glass.

On Friday morning she woke up weeping, knowing she had dreamed of her sons. The dream shimmered; faded.

Adam had already left. She squatted in front of the bedroom wardrobe and reached for the shoebox containing Robert's tapes. She emptied them into a brown manila envelope and tucked this into her briefcase. On her way in to work she went to the travel agent on Holloway Road. At lunchtime she went out with colleagues to the pub and downed three glasses of white wine. Back in college she phoned Adam at the gallery.

– I need to talk to you, but there's never time to talk at home, or else we're too tired. Shall I come and meet you after work tonight? We could go to the Wheatsheaf and have a drink.

– All right, Adam said.

His voice seemed to arrive from far away. Catherine waited. The quietness hummed between them. Once she would have been able to guess at what it meant. Now she no longer could.

– Six o'clock? Adam said: see you then.

He replaced the receiver. The line burred and chirruped. Catherine hung up. She took out Robert's four tapes and played them on the machine she had borrowed from Media Studies. She ran them back and forth, fast-forwarding then rewinding, to make sure she had missed nothing. Each one was blank. Catherine shuddered with relief. She picked up her folder of teaching notes for *Wide Sargasso Sea* and went off to her class.

Later she walked eastwards along the Strand. Cloud-roofed conduit, which swirled with rain and hurrying people. Umbrellas bobbed along the wide pavement, bumped each other like jellyfish swimming in dark water. Five thirty. The city traffic was almost at a standstill. Motorbikes could switch lanes, swerve in and out of the near-stationary vehicles with arrogant ease, but the clogging cars, vans and buses were slowed down between roadworks and red lights. Drivers hooted, crept forward, halted, hooted again.

She had left college at five sharp, to make sure of meeting Adam on time. She didn't linger as she usually did, talking to the students. She hurried off, calling farewells over her shoulder. She plunged into the tube at Tufnell Park, heading for Borough, but got on to the wrong branch of the Northern Line; suddenly realised she was at Charing Cross.

240

She erupted into the open side of the station exit facing Villiers Street, glad of what passed for fresh air, even though it was laden with diesel fumes from a taxi churning by. Gleam of the black chassis as it swung out of the railway arches, a sheet of water spraying up on either side. Jaywalkers in its path scattered, then regrouped. The station entrance was a mouth sucking up the damp crowds. They thronged in the foyer, rootling in handbags for change for the ticket machines, consulting maps, shaking the wet from their macs. Drops of water flew down on to the chequered tiled floor, crisscrossed by trails of blurred muddy footprints. To Catherine's right, the necklace of lightbulbs fringing the green awning above the stacked tiers of the flower stall glowed yellowy-pearl. Under this splashy gold the blooms arranged on the wooden planks were bright as jewels. The flowers lit up the cloudy gloom like planets. In the rain their colours shone impossibly. Bunches of blue violets on thin stems, enclosed in heart-shaped leaves, looked darkly fragile, leaning over the side of a little bucket; as though, once bought and taken into your hands, they would close up, wilt in the tarry air. Taller pots bore cellophane-wrapped mauve and white freesias, tight arrays of pink roses, trumpet sprays of orange and salmon lilies. Under a small red and white canopy a seller, perched on a long-legged stool, palmed coins with one hand and dealt out copies of the evening paper with the other. Opposite, a hawker offered cheap folding brollies. Both chanted their wares, calling out according to some internally imposed, regular rhythm, a guttural music that drowned out the weaker song of the busker strumming his guitar nearby.

Catherine turned up her padded white coat collar, so that its fur edges stroked her cheeks, and put her hands in her pockets. Hesitating; watching the rain. It fell down in straight lines, like dashes marked in pencil. As it hit the puddles underfoot it stammered into dots, was cut into curves, half-circles. A drawing made with economical gestures; quick as Morse code. The rain; the artist's pencil; both obeyed laws and both were free. She wished she were rain. It danced up and down on concrete and stone. It gurgled along kerbs, emptied itself down drains, vanished underground, like all those people making for the escalators behind her. Click of tickets; through the waist-level gates; gone.

She was lucky. She could walk to work from her new house; avoid the rush-hour press and scramble; flee the crowds. Being forced down into the tube was like being buried alive. Panic about no air, not being able to breathe. Let alone move your elbows. Getting into the lift at Tufnell Park she had felt her stomach lurch as the box of people dropped down the deep shaft. Several trains had been cancelled, or were running late; a crowd had built up on the platform. Pushed inexorably forwards by the army of shuffling commuters kneeing her from behind, she feared being swept too close to the edge, toppling over on to the live rails. You teetered; braced yourself; leaned back as forcefully as you could.

The arriving train shot in solid with bodies. The doors slid open. Like an incision in flesh; blood welling. The wall of people in the train spilt forwards, jammed nose to nose with the wall of people on the platform. Ranks of them behind, mashed together, and in front. She butted her way into the carriage, the dense mass of strangers. Their eyes, lowered in a pretence of indifference, signalled their hostility. Like it or not, you had to get intimate. Insinuate yourself between bellies, breasts. Excuse me. Excuse me. The blank-faced commuters fought back passively by refusing to move, blocking your passage with briefcases and carrier-bags. The guard's voice over the intercom barked: mind out; move along there; please. The shutting doors sealed them up; gluey squash of flesh. They were all wedged in, crammed against each other's damp raincoats, sweaty armpits, sour hair. The train jerked away, plunged into the tunnel.

After twenty minutes of jolting along, stop and start, stifling her breath as yet more passengers rammed themselves aboard, Catherine gratefully realised she was on the wrong train and fought her cramped way off, up into the open.

As soon as she stepped away from the sheltering sweetness of the flower stall, the rain hit her. She swore. Her new black suede shoes would be irreparably stained. A man shoving past stepped in a puddle, raising a spray of muddy water that splashed her white coat with streaks of dirt. If she'd had an umbrella she'd have wanted to hit him with it.

A shawled woman in a long flounced skirt, carrying a sleeping child on one arm, approached her, holding out her hand, murmuring some soft plea. She had dark hair, a gold tooth. Catherine gave her a pound and dodged past. She marched up Villiers Street and turned right. Even as she gave them money, she swivelled her eyes away from the two thin, pasty-faced girls huddled under grimy sleeping-bags in a doorway. She ignored the smiled thanks of the wild-haired young man, blanket-wrapped, who accosted her feebly from a doorway, whispering hello then pointing to his sign scrawled on cardboard. She gave him her last pound coin but refused to meet his eyes.

She wove between groups of tourists making for cafés and pubs, skipped around puddles. Alleys and courts opened off on her right, just wide enough for one person to walk through. Robert had taken her to pubs, nestled in these passageways, in the early days of her marriage, when she'd still believed she could be a go-between, put everything right between father and son, kiss it better. Robert certainly liked kissing her. He'd seize her, plant big wet ones on her mouth before she could twist her face away. She taught him to kiss her on both cheeks instead, and he taught her how to drink. In and out of all the pubs along the Strand. At the far end of these alleys: glimpses of the silver river. He rubbed his nose: Adam's bloody lucky to have you. What a disappointment that boy's been. Can't make head or tail of that nonsense he writes. Stabbing a wooden toothpick into squares of Cheddar, pouring a stream of peanuts into his mouth, coaxing her to one more Bloody Mary. She'd fold her arms, shake her head at him. His peers value Adam's work: that's all that matters. Robert said: doesn't earn much, though, does he?

Who's going to look after you in your old age? He took her about with him, squired her to shows and openings Adam refused to attend. People assumed she was his mistress and she let them. Guilt: was she betraying Adam? Complicit with Robert, yes, she was. Adam couldn't manage his old man but she could. Putty in her hands. Butter wouldn't melt in his mouth. Hugs you couldn't escape. Hands straying across breasts, knees. He thought she'd given him the right but she hadn't. Not now she was married. But she liked his gallantry, yes she did. She liked men fancying her. What was wrong with that? She realised it was Vinny she was talking to. She missed arguing with Vinny. They'd been too cool with each other for too long.

Once the boys were born Robert stopped flirting so much; settled into his role as grandfather more or less. He started to treat her again as a confidante as he lay dying. Bits and pieces of tales he whispered to her as she and Adam took turns to sit by his bed in the hospice. Visits could be made at any time: the hospice was friendlier than hospital; homelier. Death could not be tamed but here you saw it for what it was; not only the great mystery; but also ordinary. It co-existed with having your hair done and swapping photos of grandchildren and watching soap operas on TV. Vinny came in to see Robert just to relieve the other two for an hour or so now and then; he wasn't, strictly speaking, her family, after all.

Vinny was poet-in-residence for the hospice. A pilot project. Catherine had not seen her sister at work before. She watched her. Vinny hung about unobtrusively, chatted, listened a lot, tried to find out what people might require from her. If anything. She was prepared to make herself redundant. She brought in tapes and books, read poems to individual patients if that was requested, ran a writing group for ill children and another for visitors. The resulting poems were framed and hung on the yellow walls of the corridors and in the relatives' sitting-room. Catherine didn't know if Robert recognised her sister. Creative writing, he whispered: fucking therapy, more like. Tell 'em to get lost. Coughing and spitting. The sputum drooled into the plastic bowl she held under his chin.

He told Catherine stories he had not told her before. Images from wartime broke loose from his memory mosaic and clattered on to the blanket. He summoned the dead. The stinking hills of corpses he had had to clamber over at Dunkirk to get to the beach; they were squelching and soft; your boots sank into their eyes and mouths. The officers who kicked their men out of sheltering doorways and took their places and then got blown up anyway. Real as ghosts, those people packed into air-raid shelters; sleeping in the tubes, laid out in rows on the platforms; preparing to be dead. That was why he hated travelling by Underground. He breathed harshly. The air scraped in and out of his wrecked lungs. The flesh on his neck bunched in folds. Towards the end he stopped talking, had to concentrate on vomiting; on bearing the pain. He rejected pain relief as long as possible. Why? That was how he was going to do things, that was all. That was how he had been brought up. He was afraid of morphine; that he would become addicted. So what? Catherine thought. Sometimes Adam could not bear to see his father suffer so much and had to go out, into the corridor. How could you watch someone suffer like that, he said to Catherine afterwards, and know you were powerless to relieve them? Finally Robert was persuaded by the gentle staff to accept morphine.

Sometimes, if Adam wasn't in the room, Catherine held Robert's hand. She wanted to accompany him as far as she possibly could into the black tunnel that was opening up. Not to die herself, but to go with him as far as she could so that he would not feel afraid.

What a liar she was. When it came to it she couldn't do it. She was a coward and she failed. Whenever he had begun to whisper to her about his ex-wife, about his love for her, about his affairs with all those girls, she had interrupted him, changed the subject. He had wanted to unburden his soul but she had not let him. Call for a priest if you want but don't tell me. Do your deathbed repentance scene somewhere else. I don't want to know.

Now she had decided to tell Adam something of what had gone on between Robert and herself. In turn, to try and make her confession. Sooner or later, with the show coming up, with so much attention being focused on Robert's paintings, he would work it out. She ought to tell him before he guessed. Perhaps she was simply being selfish and egotistical. She would hurt him. Perhaps she should shut up, as she had done for years. From half a mile away she heard the sonorous bells of St Paul's boom out the three-quarter hour.

She ploughed along the Strand. How did you find the words to say it? Open your hands and I'll give you a present. A stream of red geranium petals? Red coral beads? No: a shower of red-hot cinders from the fire. His palms would be scarred.

She remembered that sequence of pictures in the chapel at school. The smiling angel who seized the lance, with its glowing tip, and pressed it into the centre of the saint's outstretched hands; then into his sides; into his feet. Pain inflicted thus was a gift from God. But I'm no sadist, not really, she whispered to Adam walking invisibly at her side: and I didn't tell you because I didn't want you to be upset, that's all.

Liar. She was afraid he wouldn't love her if he knew. He was strictly moral about some things. Was it really a lie when you tried to protect someone from being hurt? She'd kept her side of the secret and she'd known Robert would keep his. He enjoyed sharing a secret concealed from his son.

She'd played at being the arrogant, enraptured saint. Robert had desired her and she'd believed she'd been singled out; marked; set apart from other women. She was God's chosen girl. Like Mary Immaculate. She'd believed she was both angel and woman, able to bear the Saviour's wounds and be glad of them. Like those mystics, those hysterics who embraced the stigmata. These saints surrounded her now and chanted that she was one of them. Like the cherubim inflicting the red marks of the nails they each had six pairs of wings. They were outlined in flames and they were laughing because they loved pain. The martyrs had welcomed pain too, going towards it with outstretched hands. At school she had wanted to emulate their heroism. Of course she had. And all she'd ended up doing was writing texts to entertain young businesswomen who believed they had to be punished for having some power. That was Vinny's view of her writing. They'd discussed it just once, when Catherine had had one glass of wine too many. Catherine had sworn Vinny to silence. And in particular don't tell Adam. The novellas had been a container for her secret feelings. They'd kept her good and her marriage safe. So she was perfectly justified in writing them, she said to the Vinny who lived in her head. But Vinny did not reply.

Catherine felt plunged into endless night. Part of a procession filing towards increasing darkness. Carried along in the stream of office workers making towards Fleet Street for Blackfriars, she'd almost forgotten where she was going. Gloomy afternoon; the sun hidden behind grey clouds. The rain was easing off. Just drizzle now. People on every side. She wanted to walk for ever with these people and never arrive. She wanted just to drift in this mighty current, wash up somewhere far away, where there would be no more suffering. She felt very lonely despite being part of the hurrying crowd. Adam and she seemed to have stopped loving each other. There was no love left; and she would have to go away, far away from him, unable to reach him. She was mourning the loss of her love. Nothing but darkness inside her. Nothing but emptiness. She was made of nothing but grief. Grief stabbed her in the belly and she contorted, clutching at herself, unable to still the pain. Tears burst out of her. She dissolved into the rain. Tears and rain poured down her face. So this was the end. All that love was gone. Finished. Love ran out and that was that.

She could not stop crying. She bent her head, so that passers-by would not notice. She would have to leave Adam, as he seemed already to have left her, and go off alone somewhere and live in the desert. She was so lonely. She didn't know what to do except keep walking.

The old Catherine had tried to keep herself apart, a cool step away from most other people; she'd stayed safe, intact; but that Catherine was gone, melted into the rain, mixed up now with all the people around her; there was just this sad woman who wept and went on walking along. As thousands had done before her, thousands of people in all the centuries gone by. Other people in the past had walked here, crying and wretched; she was one of them, part of their company, part of a great stream of the dead; she was joined to all those other people suffering; she was not separate from them at all but merged with them; walking along the Strand and crying. The dead who had walked here before her were walking with her now and they were alive because she could feel their presence, pressing close about her. All of them going along together in the dark rain. So she did not have to be lonely and she did not have to be alone; she had to plunge in and be with all the others, and love them; it was that simple. Sorrow was a sort of knowledge; strange how grief delivered you back into the world. She discovered that her parents were beside her, walking along with her. The tears broke out of her like stones.

Once, aged seven or so, Adam had hidden under the table in the hall. Wintry lino. A draught snaking in from under the front door to coil around his ankles. Choking smell of hard-boiled eggs and furniture polish. First he tried the hatstand, with its drop of woollen coats, and then he crawled in under the table and waited there, hands clasping his knees. He wanted to feel enclosed, and he wanted to see out, and he wanted to have space around him. The table stood over him, sturdy as a cow sheltering its calf. He called it hiding, but he wanted to be found. He chose a place where his mother would notice him. No point hiding if she didn't find you. A key clinked outside, fitted itself into the lock. The front door swung at him like a fist, and his mother's high heels stepped briskly in. What are you doing there? Don't be silly. Come out right away. She chased him into the kitchen to have his tea.

– Adam, are you okay? Charlie asked.

– No, but I will be soon, Adam said.

He donned his jacket. Just let me murder my wife and I'll be fine. Just let me grind this chisel into her lovely face.

– Let's go for a drink, Charlie said.

Adam waved him away.

He sat in a pub on Queen Victoria Street. A banal place, walled in engraved plate glass, full of young men and women in suits shouting at each other over booming music. He had a sense that Charlie had followed him, to keep an eye on him. Why? He drank large vodkas and thought about Vinny.

In his dream six nights ago she'd held something hidden in her palm. A secret. Show me, he'd begged: tell me what it is. Now she gave it to him, cruel girl. Impossible to grasp. Spiny as a clump of newly fallen sweet chestnuts you try to pick up with ungloved hands. A crack in the thorny case shows a hint of white fur lining, silky curve of the dark brown nut. First you think beautiful then you think dangerous.

She'd made it all up. Storyteller. She was pathetic. Mad.

Adam had downed three large vodkas. He bought himself a fourth. He knew he must be drunk by now but he felt as coldly empty as the space under a table. He was a cube of air. The air began to collapse because there was nothing to hold it, give it a shape. He needed a covering; an outside.

He tried to get back in control. He made a mental list. One. He was upset because his wife had wanked in front of his father, he presumed she had, and let the old goat watch. Two. He was upset because presumably she had pretended this was all in the cause of art. Three. He was upset because she'd never told him. That was lying by default. Four. He was upset because she had been writing pornography in secret and hadn't told him that either. Five. He was upset because if she had let Robert fuck her then he was destroyed because she had held him up, held him together, sworn she loved him, yet all this time she had been mocking him.

He hated Catherine so much that he knew his skin had been stripped off. He was raw. What you do to animals when you butcher them. Pierce them with your knife then tug off their hides. Marsyas was hung upside-down and flayed alive by Apollo. The angry god punished him; tore off his flesh; peeled him like a fruit. With your surface lost you were gone for ever. Nothing but agony. Blood springing out. He was filmed all over with blood: it seeped from his eyeballs and ran down his face. He clutched with his arms to keep himself in. He tried to bandage his leaks with his hands.

He got up and left the pub. Six o'clock on a May evening. The rain had stopped. A fresh breeze tossed the little waves on the river, which glittered in the sudden sun and reflected the blue of the sky. First of all he plunged down on to the little strip of shingle at Queenhythe where he had met Vinny a week ago. Standing on the filth-strewn beach he couldn't decide where to go. He was supposed to meet Catherine in the Wheatsheaf, but there were no words he could speak to her and so he had to protect her from what his hands wanted to do instead. Beat her face to a pulp. It was impossible to be with anyone. He was too dangerous. He might kill anyone who spoke to him.

He climbed up on to the walkway that went past the back of the Vintners' Building. He left that wounded son, that poor sack of blood, behind him, at Queenhythe. Vinny could have it. Pecking bird. Scavenger. It wasn't him, that lump of red rubbish; hacked purplish steak. He'd been disembowelled and his heart torn out, his guts and liver and spleen tossed contemptuously down on to the pebbles, where they lay and hurt because they were still alive.

But he had been transformed. Now he was made of metal. Now he had grown a coat of spikes. Keep off. He was a clanking pylon-giant. He couldn't fold himself up to fit inside a pub. Ridiculous.

He walked on to Southwark Bridge. He felt he ought to stop half-way because he always did and people said life had to go on. He leaned against the parapet. Passers-by, tourists, commuters hurrying for trains dodged round him. He gazed down at the scurrying water far below. Then he climbed up on to the turquoise-painted parapet. Slightly domed in the middle. Slippery from the recent rain. He had to concentrate to keep his balance.

When the bough breaks the baby shall fall. Once he'd been a baby and Robert had held him in his arms and had not dropped him but swung him to and fro and cradled him. Robert was gone. Pages torn out of his best book never to be replaced. Everything he'd ever been: offered up to Robert; oh please love me. If Robert was gone then Adam was gone too. But he was cunning. He could get Adam back. You just had to read what the river said.

The waves rippled along like the lines of an untidy manuscript. They scribbled as fast as handwriting. A new, watery language. He could read it easily. Simple stuff, like a child's ABC. A book of instructions written in water. How to live. You had to give yourself to life, as you gave yourself when making love. You had not to be afraid. You had to leap into the abyss of nothingness and then words would come, the angel would come. He rode upon the cherubim and did fly;

he came flying upon the wings of the wind; he made darkness his secret place; and thick clouds to cover him. Adam started laughing. The clarity was as brilliant as when he used to drop acid and it burned to you: what you knew but had forgotten. You had to embrace the air, which had the angel hidden in it. The angel would catch you and you could not fall but fly.

Someone shouted his name. He turned. Catherine was walking towards him from the northern side of the bridge. The sun caught her hair, a burning halo. She'd tried to hold him up but she couldn't any longer she was too tired she would have to let go. Hang on Adam hang on. Charlie was striding towards him as well. Shimmering in the light. Outlined in gold. Making towards him as purposefully as soldiers or as police. Coming to arrest him. Stop, Adam. Stop. Wait.

He teetered. No time to be lost. He wasn't drunk. Not really. He didn't want to fall off of course not.

They were yelling at him.

Of course they were right.

Rescue me.

He needed to get down. He lifted one foot. He slipped on the curved surface of the parapet. He put his foot down again. The soles of his boots lost their grip and he lost his balance he stretched out his arms he jumped up to the high angel roof he flew.

PART FIFTEEN

Autumn is a time of year your favourite poets associate with loss and death, is it not, *cher* Monsieur? How many long, dull stanzas did you not force us to commit to memory and then recite out loud to you in class? For you, however, in reality, autumn in Brussels was an invigorating season: your chance to display your powers afresh at the start of the new school term; new lectures to prepare; new lessons to plan; new pupils to cajole, hector, dazzle, reward with the occasional fond word or caress.

But my second year at your school was my first without Emily, and so my heart grew heavier as the autumn months wore on. It was one thing to be a pupil there with her; quite another to have returned alone as a pupil-teacher. Difficult to struggle against the melancholy produced by the dank chill of those early mornings, the wind sweeping the streets scuffing the last plane leaves into the gutter, the bandstand abandoned and silent in the park, the grey mist wreathing the house. It rained a lot, insistent rain that penetrated the thickest boots and gusted under hats and umbrellas. I'd come in, damp skirts clinging to my knees, from an errand or a walk in town, and stand shivering in the cold tiled hallway, listening to the sounds of merriment issuing from behind the door to the salon where you played with your children. Close to you, doubtless, Madame Heger sat by serenely with her embroidery, supervising you all, making sure your games did not become too boisterous and rough, to the possible detriment of her china ornaments balanced on flimsy three-legged tables.

I saw far less of you than formerly. Now that I was helping to teach, and not simply learning, our schedules clashed; I could no longer, for example, attend your composition class as often as I wished. You and Madame Heger both invited me to use your salon as my own, to join you there in the evenings; but I could not let myself intrude on your domestic sanctum, your sacred pleasures with your children. So, at any rate, I declared in my letters home.

What a liar I was. I was too jealous, that's all; I couldn't bear witnessing your happiness as you romped and laughed, your wife benevolently looking on. Instead I banished myself; I condemned myself, bad girl, to detention. After I'd finished preparing my teaching work for the next day in the rapidly darkening classroom I'd eat my supper with the others in the refectory. Then, leaving the pupils to their evening recreation, study, and *lecture pieuse*, I'd go upstairs to my cubicle in the cold, silent dormitory, with a candle, and spend my evening up there alone, sitting on my bed, my hands wrapped in my sleeves, the end of my nose icy and raw, my heart sick and full of dread for the future. It was clear to me that one day soon I'd have to leave. Madame Heger would make sure she got rid of me; in the nicest possible way. It would be for my own benefit; I'd thank her for it one day; my own good sense should tell me that. With her voice pitter-pattering in my ears like the rain I'd undress and say my prayers, lie awake shivering, pray for sleep.

Here, in Nohant, the autumn weather has been warm enough for us to continue lunching out of doors, to take walks, to go on picnics. This afternoon I went mushrooming with Madame Sand and her grandchildren. She was expecting a visitor to arrive later on, and wanted something delicious to serve him for supper. We put on sturdy boots and armed ourselves with walking-sticks, and long flat baskets made by Thomas, woven of split hazel twigs. Over our crinolines we tied on thick linen aprons borrowed from the cook.

We took the trap and drove to the woods. We unhitched the mare and tied her loosely to a tree, left her cropping the grass at the edge of the road, plunged into green-gold darkness. The children ran about playing hide-and-seek but Madame Sand was hunting seriously. She spotted our fat treasures first almost every time, pouncing with cries of triumph. She kept exulting at how many I missed: oh, you didn't see these but I did; I've got the eyes of a lynx.

She was laughing with pleasure at our freedom to explore wherever we wanted. She told me a tale of her youth in Paris, when she dressed as a man in order to go to the theatre on her own, roam the boulevards without fear of being harassed and attacked. I told her how I sent out my books in a similar masculine disguise. No false gallantry, therefore, had afflicted either of us. Though both of us had to endure plenty of insults once our deception was uncovered.

My hostess could talk and mushroom-hunt at the same time. She concentrated on the task in hand, sharp eyes cast down, swerving around. I thought of Emily: how much she would have enjoyed this expedition. It hurts less to remember her than it once did; she's inside me now; we cannot be parted ever again. Aurore cried to me: you're off in a dream. No wonder she found more mushrooms. Six to every one of mine.

So we circled back to the horse and trap and drove home, the sun in the west blinding our eyes, Aurore shouting that she couldn't see a thing but going at her usual speed anyway. She does it to amuse the little ones, who love being scared. We bumped up and down over muddy ruts, nearly jumping out of our seats, holding on tight. Aurore went straight down to the kitchen, to confer with the cook about how best to present our finds. The two of them are often in dispute and this occasion was like many others I have witnessed. Their voices erupted at the top of the kitchen stairs. Grilled. No: fried with garlic and parsley. No: simmered in cream. No: baked in pastry.

I came into the salon with the children and lit the fire laid ready waiting in the grate, and I sat by it, smelling the scent of the logs, and felt a fizz between my shoulder-blades, like a taste of sweetness, almost an ache, which was the happiness of the afternoon in the woods with Aurore flowing on into the happiness of wanting to share it with you, like a piece of

262

honeycomb broken off that I could offer you, a gold crust dripping with sugar. And so I thought of you peacefully and I embraced your absence and wished you all joy.

I shall toss this letter into the fire eventually. A burnt offering. Unlike the mushrooms, which bubbled quietly in a bath of hot butter, a splash of white wine, on the stove in the kitchen below, and then were brought upstairs in a pink china dish. Madame Sand's visitor, her friend Monsieur Flaubert (the novelist), ate two helpings. So did I. He departed this morning. His presence put us *en fête*. We ate well, we drank good wine, we polkaed and waltzed, we played Charades, we went for walks, we frolicked in the garden with the children, we strummed the piano and sang. Monsieur Flaubert dressed up as a woman one night and danced the chahucha. Accordingly I donned a cravat and waistcoat and twirled opposite him.

The highlight of the entertainment, as far as the children were concerned, were the plays with the puppets that we wrote and performed. Have I mentioned the puppets? Aurore's son Maurice converted one of the smaller downstairs salons into a puppet theatre some time ago, with curtains and painted scenery, and carved many puppet-actors, representing a range of characters, comic to tragic to grotesque.

Watching the puppets jerk and dance from their strings I was reminded of my father's story of how, when we were small, he lined us up in front of him in his study, and handed us masks, which he bade us hold up before our faces. We were to speak through these masks in answer to his questions. This was done with the best of intentions, in order to lessen our nervousness in being addressed by such a tall, imposing personage as himself, and so to encourage us to give our true opinions. Accordingly, we spoke. When asked what a child most lacked, we answered: age and experience. What to do with a naughty boy? Reason with him, and if he won't listen to reason then whip him. What's the difference between the intellects of men and women? Men's are stronger than women's, as their bodies are. What's the best book in the world? The Bible. He was proud of these replies, and recorded them in a note, considering that they evinced remarkable evidence of our precocious understanding.

I have no memory of this experience. It was my father's legend he handed to us, his formative myth of our early years. All these years later, I wonder now whether we little children really did speak as we felt or as we already knew, by that subtle intelligence infants develop very young of the needs of their elders and betters, our father required? We reportedly gave him, after all, the correct answers; ones he could approve of. Could we, so young, have dared to speak otherwise? Not inside the house, that's certain; not in Father's study; and not in the parlour, where Aunt ruled. In the kitchen, with Tabby, we were free to a certain extent. We teased and mocked her, rude little beasts that we were. And in bed at night, as I told you before, we made up our own plays and spoke our own lines.

Outside, on the moors, we ran completely wild. Played

dangerous games, fought each other, had adventures, took mad risks. That's where my mind grew and took flight: in our complete freedom outside the house; out on the open, unpeopled moors. And so when Aunt came to live with us, to care for us and teach us better, that's when we had to invent our magical kingdoms over which only children ruled, where only children's imaginations held sway. Emily managed to hold on to her inner kingdom and never left it. The rest of us were born bitterly into the real world.

My dear, good father. Have I gone on speaking to him from behind a mask, like a character in a play? Like a girl in a story? Is that how I talked to Arthur too?

Who wrote my story and described the devoted daughter, good wife, hard-working teaching assistant, devout church-goer? Who fitted me in? A fiction, all of it, on one level, however compelling; however convenient sometimes. Yes: a mask I hid myself behind. Cowardly Charlotte. But I was schooled at Cowan Bridge, remember. I learned early on to starve, to long hopelessly for maternal kindness, to freeze. Later, in your school, Monsieur, I learned that the love I wanted was forbidden. So I gave up asking. I wanted only in secret, and converted my desires into means of self-punishment. Only when I wrote novels did I invent my own mask. Telling sanctioned lies, writing fiction, I could fly free of nice Charlotte the good daughter. I could write of rage and of pain. I wrote about teeth grating on stones, about scorpions clutched in the palm. I rehearsed different lives. I imagined alternative selves. I discovered what it felt like to be someone else.

That person dwelling neatly in the parsonage at Haworth, as fixed and predictable as a book of etiquette, was only the ghost of my real live self. I've left my double behind, an effigy cold and correct as a corpse, to tend to Arthur and Papa, while I frolic with Madame Sand and talk to you, my dear Monsieur. My true self dresses up and dances, is born from moment to moment, changes as feelings change, as words and desires flow in conversation. My true self dances the chahucha, goes mushroom-hunting in the woods, wants to write another novel.

What's the best book in the world? The one not written yet. It waits in the darkness. Like a ghost. Like the unborn.

My first book came out of darkness.

We were in Manchester together in the darkened room, my father and I. He could not see me and that was the whole point: he was blind; we'd gone there for the cataract operation to be performed. I was present while it was done, as he requested, and afterwards he lay for weeks very quietly and resignedly in the darkness, waiting for his sight to return. And what did I do? I wrote, of course. I started *Jane Eyre*. I wrote because he could not see me; he was still blind; and that freed me; in that state of freedom I could write.

Must I blind him again if I am to write again? Oh, my poor father: no wonder I had to flee Haworth in order not to blind you a second time; in order to write I believed I had to murder you.

Do you know why I fell in love with you, *mon cher* Monsieur? I admired you, certainly: your ardent intellect, your honesty, your beauty. You were young; not much older than I; bursting with vigorous life. But also I believed that from the beginning you knew me; you recognised me; you saw me, the woman, the artist; you looked at me affectionately; you called me by my true name.

All too soon you had to vanish; I would turn you to stone; you put up your shield; you backed away; you disappeared.

Madame Sand sees me.

Last night I saw her and Monsieur Flaubert.

I was very thirsty and the carafe on the washstand was empty. I tiptoed downstairs in the darkness. The study door was slightly ajar. A seesaw of voices. I peeped in. There they both were, armchairs pulled up to the fire, feet up on the fender, dashing at it hammer and tongs, that ardent discussion on literature they'd begun earlier and which quite clearly would keep them going half the night. Now Aurore was no longer the gracious hostess, the kind grandmother; she was not in the salon any longer, in public view; now she was simply his friend the writer, as ferocious as he. They were in disagreement, arguing out their differences over a nightcap, frowning and smiling both at once; passionate; trying not to interrupt each other too much; enjoying themselves.

He got up to pour them both more brandy. He glanced over at the door and saw me. He winked. I fled. I filled my carafe in the kitchen and came back up here to bed.

Goodnight, dear master. Thank you for listening. Time to tear this up and burn it and sleep. Time to think about returning home.

PART SIXTEEN

The day after meeting Adam in the Flora café, Vinny left for France on the early boat. She got up at four a.m. and sped along empty roads to Portsmouth like a criminal making a getaway.

She reached Sainte-Madeleine after lunch in a *routier*, stopping on the outskirts of Sainte-Marthe for petrol and provisions. Since last year a tree-surrounded field had been levelled, scalped. The new supermarket bristled up, a long, single-storey, marigold-yellow prefab on the main road, with a plate-glass door and no windows. Shiny and hard-edged, it crouched like a beetle in its huge car-park, glittering gravelled tarmac bordered with neat beds of ranked orange, blue and pink pansies and primulas surrounding oblongs of scarlet shrub roses. No rest for the eye; you felt tired looking at such bright, bony plants. Somebody had tried to soften the environment, had made an effort at adornment, but the effect remained harsh. The flowers and bushes needed green around them and there was none.

The little back road out of Sainte-Madeleine was busy with tractors. The hedgerow trees almost met overhead. She swung right at the dumpy stone cross with the empty niche at its heart. Formerly a porcelain statue of the Virgin had lodged there, tolerated by Robert because it was old, but it had been stolen two years ago. Vinny's hands were suddenly clammy on the wheel. In all these years of coming to visit Jeanne for the occasional long weekend, she had never gone back to Les Deux Saintes. She had preferred not to. She had walked past the bottom of the lane and never turned up it. She had avoided visiting during the school holidays, so that she did not overlap with Adam and Catherine. Once Robert had transformed the house into a *gîte*, Jeanne earned some extra money by acting as caretaker, held the keys for the tourists who came to stay, but Vinny had never accompanied her to help settle the guests in. No thanks. I'll get the supper on instead. This time she had decided to sleep at Les Deux Saintes, to spend the days there on her own. Jeanne was offended; had to be smoothed down.

The steep bank on the left-hand side of the lane waved with patches of nettles, white clumps of greater stitchwort and Solomon's seal, stands of dark pink foxgloves and white daisies nodding above green ferns. She accelerated up the slope, turned the last bend, and halted.

The house was knee-deep in feathery grass. The tops of two lilacs rose up out of this green excess and foamed whiteness to one side of the blue slate roof. The low building was like an animal collapsed fast asleep. Almost hidden in its pasture. Perhaps the Sleeping Beauty had looked like that; comfortable as a cow. All rumpled and flung down and not caring; slumped bones under a velvet coat.

Faded lavender paint peeled from the closed shutters; blue blisters and blue cracks. Unlocked, the parched blue door did not budge. Vinny's shoulders remembered what you had to do; she leaned against it until it squeaked open, scraping on the tiled floor. She stepped forwards into the darkness, turned sideways, groped for the window catches, and opened the windows. She unbolted the shutters, pushed them wide. Sunlight flung itself through the gap, bleached walls and floor.

Catherine had said the house had not been let since Christmas. Vinny was an intruder barging in, startling the spiders in residence. Big black ones skittered on fat hairy legs into the corners. Smaller ones folded their limbs and hid in their webs. Smell of dust. The house felt powdery-dry. Cobwebs blurred the angles of the walls and swung in furry swags between the rafters.

She went back out into the garden, descended the steps into the front orchard. A green sea. Crickets rasped: the sound of heat. Horseflies from the cows in the field circled her head. The grass was waist-high. She pushed into it like a swimmer, parting it in front of her with both hands. She moved slowly through its dry fragrance. Tall stalks rustled about her, bent open in her wake. The branches of the cherry made a green tracery overhead. Rags of blue sky were patched in between the jagged edges of the leaves. The former *potager* had disappeared. The grass had closed over it and swallowed it up. In the centre of the orchard a tall hawthorn waved unruly arms.

She turned and slowly forced a path back. Sweet-smelling greenery tickled her nose; showers of seeds sprayed out; waves of stored sun. A perfect hiding-place for children to build dens in. A hot and aromatic wilderness that snakes would adore.

The thought of snakes made her retreat to the van. She took out her bags and groceries, carried them inside.

Catherine had given her a list of small items of furniture to bring back, as well as crockery and books. But before packing, she cleaned. She spent the first three days at it. She opened all the windows and doors and played music very loud and set to, sweeping and dusting, washing and polishing.

She enjoyed the transformation she effected. Long ago she'd discovered there was no point doing housework every day, the way she'd been brought up. Baths and sinks, perhaps, but the rest could go its own sweet way. You had to let a house get dirty in order to demonstrate and enjoy its metamorphosis from grubby hovel into sunlit airy space smelling of flowers and beeswax and soap. The house a palimpsest: layers of memories of what it was like before; its clotted grime and filth. Other people's dirt always seemed worse than one's own: there was an extra, aggressive pleasure in getting rid of it. Housework could also be enjoyably narcissistic: cherishing the house you cherished yourself. Catherine had found that out years back. The only annoying thing about housework was if you felt forced to do it and then taken for granted.

Vinny did like the order and bareness she achieved: a big jug of white daisies set on a piece of lace-edged linen on the gleaming table, the neat piles of books, the shining mirrors. All very creditable and satisfying. But also she loved and remembered the mess and squalor that existed before: the spiders' webs and dead flies and crusts of mud and tufts of fluff. The outdoors trying to come in and take over. She liked the way nature wanted to invade; to swallow up the house. She wanted to give it a good chance before she fought back. Who on earth aspired towards domestic sanctity, a perfect interior? Vinny did the important things and let everything else slide. But because Catherine and Adam were paying her to be conscientious she cleaned more elaborately for them than she did at home. In her novels Mrs Gaskell sang the pleasures of exquisite cleanliness; of old chintz much-washed; in her biography of Charlotte she commented approvingly on her friend's tidy parlour. But Charlotte had had a servant to help her, and Mrs Gaskell several. Vinny almost achieved the Gaskell standard of perfection once a year, which was quite enough.

By the end of Thursday, the sitting-room and kitchen were immaculate. The upstairs could wait. Vinny rinsed off her sweat and grime under the feeble shower Robert had had installed in the bathroom shed, put on her favourite long blue linen dress, poured herself a glass of *pays-de-Loire* Gamay. After her picnic supper outside, she lit a fire and set candles on the high stone mantelpiece. She left the front door open, so that she could watch the sky deepen to radiant indigo, the stars emerge, the moon rise. Darkness here was as friendly and good as your favourite black cat slinking in; you could let it flow into the house and not be too separate.

She pulled up a basket-chair, kicked off her espadrilles, propped her bare feet on the brick hearth. She sat with her hands folded over the novel and the exercise-book in her lap. But she was not in the mood for reading or writing. Memories unfolded their wings and flew about like bats. That girl she'd been, standing in the moonlit garden smelling of fresh damp earth, peeping in. She saw that girl again, looking in from the outside; wishing passionately to belong somewhere; imagining an older self that might one day have a house and feel at home. She hadn't quite managed it. No lover at the moment, either. No children. Impossible to have borne Adam's child: he'd left her. And none of the men she'd loved since had wanted children. Yet she'd lived the writer's life she'd aimed for when she was young. That was something. She'd made sacrifices. That was all right. She'd chosen them.

She unrolled quilts on to a row of cushions, for a bed in front of the fire, as she'd done on the previous two evenings. When she fell asleep she dreamed of snakes roaming the upstairs rooms, slithering in through gaps in the eaves, rustling in the ceiling just overhead.

She huddled next to the cold fire. Glad of the dawn scorching in through the open shutters, the cacophony of birds. She put her overalls back on and continued her cleaning. All day she worked, moving through the converted *grenier*. The roof up here was perfectly sound; no gaps to invite wriggling snakes. Nonetheless, she needed to exorcise something. From one of the sheds she took a ladder, a paintbrush, a pot of gold paint. She laid the ladder across the hole in the floorboards of the middle attic, then stood on it to paint a message in flowing gold script along the beam dividing the space in two. For love is as strong as death. Then she returned downstairs, picked up a cushion and a bottle of wine and went outside.

Tonight she was due to have supper down the road with Jeanne and her husband Lucien. Two of her oldest friends. She needed a shower, to wash her hair, change her clothes. First of all, though, grubby and sweaty as she was, she lounged on the front step, sipping a glass of Muscadet. This was her favourite place, she had discovered, half in and half out of the house, half in and half out of the garden. You hovered, part of both. Able to enjoy both at the same time. The house braced her back and the garden opened before her.

Laziness. No need to move. She looked dreamily down the lane. No-one around. The self could be let go, could dissolve, flow out, merge with the landscape. Looser, larger. A sort of hovering attention that floated like a net. Smell of cut grass ripening to hay. The sun of early evening washed the air with gold and warmed her face. Three cows lay in the meadow opposite under an apple tree. Very faintly, borne on the breeze from the village, came the sound of the church bells ringing the Angelus. A cockerel crowed.

A flicker of blue. Someone was moving about down in the orchard.

She stood up, in order to see better over the low hedge.

Adam. He was making his way slowly through the tousled fringes of grass, like a swimmer, just as she had, three days earlier, when she first arrived.

He hadn't noticed her. He was wearing his old blue jeans, a blue T-shirt, a soft tweed jacket. His hands were shoved into his pockets.

She could not move or speak. Why had he come unannounced to France? Perhaps he regretted allowing her into the house, thought her an intruder, an interloper? Perhaps he'd come to berate her for her behaviour five days ago? She hadn't yet felt brave enough to ring and apologise. No use doing it too soon, falsely, just to get yourself out of trouble. Besides, what did you say? The words might be stored somewhere deep down; but they had not yet surfaced. That conversation might have been killed stone-dead. She wasn't sure.

He didn't look angry or hostile in the least. The expression on his face was puzzled. He seemed older, and fragile, as though he'd been ill. Perhaps that was it. Perhaps he'd suddenly felt the need for escape, for some sort of holiday.

She wanted to start forward and call his name but she was afraid of startling him. As though he were a deer stepping quietly out of the woods on to the road and you must freeze or he'll leap away. She held her breath and stood stock still.

Adam looked up and saw her. His face broke into a faint, abstracted smile. Surprised, she greeted him.

– Hello.

He did not reply. He looked back at her patiently. Hello, yes, you are there, but I'm busy thinking, please don't interrupt. Vinny thought: am I dreaming this? Her mind, darting to and fro, clutched at a solution. He must have parked the car down the lane, out of sight of the house, immediately fallen asleep after his long journey, and begun dreaming. Something earlier on must have upset him and so now he was sleepwalking.

You were not supposed to waken sleepwalkers. Perhaps she could coax him back towards the house.

Adam averted his gaze from hers and moved forward again, wading through the green waves rippling about him. Then he stopped under the wild hawthorn in the centre of the orchard. His eyelids shuttered down. The blue flash of his eyes was gone.

She hesitated. Surely she should go down to him. Try and get him to come back up to the house.

Something caught her by the arms and immobilised her. Telling the tale to Jeanne and Lucien over supper, later that evening, she tried to describe the forbidding impulse, its authority and power. Like that story in the Bible of wrestling with the angel. You want to move forward but he won't let you. An angel's grip is so much stronger than your own.

Seeing her friends' shrugging incomprehension she tried again. Like being an escaped heifer, backed into the corner of the lane, then tapped with long sticks to run in the direction the farmer wants. Your own will, however imperious, doesn't matter nearly as much as the skill of the other to thwart you.

Like having a halter flung over your head. Being lassoed suddenly. Caught by invisible bonds; constrained.

He must be in some sort of trouble. She shifted from foot to foot. She felt her hands lift into the air, reach out towards him. Some physical force wanted to spill out of her, flow across the orchard and gently touch his face. She pulled her hands back. Down to her sides. She forced them to hold on to her overalls.

Adam shimmered in the heat. Slowly he began to dissolve. Then he vanished.

– You mean it was like one of the little ones having a dream, Jeanne said: waking up, not knowing it's not real.

– This is real, Lucien said.

He poured Vinny another glass of wine.

After supper she kissed them both goodnight and walked back to Les Deux Saintes. She perched outside on the front step in the moonlight and thought about Robert.

They'd talked one afternoon at the hospice, when Robert was alone and Vinny had looked in on him as she was passing. She sat with him for a while. He was fiddling with his tape recorder, swearing because it wasn't working properly. He ended up talking to her instead. He abandoned the machine and lay back against his pillows.

– She was a good model, your sister, he said: she could hold a pose well, she was strong, and she was so beautiful. She was proud of how beautiful she was. She loved taking her clothes off for me. She was in it too, as much as I was. I adored her. I'd never have hurt her.

He had his eyes half closed. The lids were drooping and lashless. The hands dropped on the turned-back edge of sheet were covered in brown spots.

Vinny said: I looked in through the studio door one day and saw you both. I was curious, because you never allowed us in. So I decided to have a look.

A hot afternoon. Adam had slumped asleep in a knot of sheets. She had pulled on clothes, gone downstairs, wandered through the garden in search of her sister. Seeing the studio door ajar, she had crept forward to peer round it. She remembered the absolute, silent concentration of the man and the girl. Her sun-reddened knees. The white fire of sunlight burning through the muslin blinds on to the back of his head, burnishing his curls. A fly buzzing. With a great effort of will she stopped the picture moving. She reduced it to a flat image in two dimensions; a study in shadows. What she had seen was private. She didn't mention it to Catherine afterwards. She had slunk away and gone into the dark kitchen to fetch a beer.

She and Robert sat together in silence. The room was very warm. Vinny was sweating. The plastic seat of her chair stuck to her jeans. Robert whispered that he was tired. Soon he fell into a doze. He was mumbling. The words drifted together; incomprehensible. His hands lifted and played in the air. The morphine did that.

Vinny remained beside him for a while, not wanting to disturb him by moving away too quickly. His hands looked as though they were searching. Like the hands of the trapeze artist as he launches himself towards the swinging rope oppo-site, on the other side of the whistling empty air. As though he wanted to fly off and just go.

No, Vinny thought. That's me. Wanting to be done with all this. Selfish cow. Whereas, more uncomfortably, death came in fits and starts and could not be rushed and sitting with the dying that was what you learned. You suffered because they suffered but that was your problem; to be held back. They needed you to walk along with them, and fit in with them, and let them take their required time. Their hard journey was theirs and you should not interrupt it. Your own sorrow could get in the way. You had to take sorrow off, like a child screaming and kicking in your arms, and deal with it elsewhere. The dying simply needed you to be a witness; a companion. They were not there to cheer you up and apologise for dying. They concentrated. They had a job to do and wanted you to let them get on with it. Sometimes, in this hospice where pain relief was so skilfully administered, this job involved talking and telling stories. Sometimes your job was to help the dying people feel con-nected with all those who had gone before, and all those who were left. One of the roles of the poet was to reconnect with the past; with history. But mostly you just had to be there; shut up and listen; prompt only when required. People dying were not on stage; did not make beautiful heartrending speeches. Their last words were about ordi-nary things. That was the point.

Robert's forehead gleamed. The dome of the skull lifted

the stretched skin. Elsewhere the mottled flesh sagged. Collapsed cheeks; loose jowls. His body seemed wrinkled away. Little and shrunken. How incongruous to see him like this, an old man in pyjamas, captured by illness; when in her memory he had remained that sunburnt, burly god; erupting out of the studio bullying and bellowing; that curly-haired host shouting for more wine; laughing. She'd found him sexy as well as overbearing. She hadn't been able to admit that to herself then. She had felt too frightened. Catholic girls didn't fancy father-figures; you were supposed to sublimate sexy feelings into loving God. Incestuous desires were the worst of all. You were lost. You were the whore. All terribly dramatic stuff. Ridiculous. She wanted to laugh. She wanted to cry. She wanted to take that anguished adolescent she'd been, that awkward twenty-five-year-old, into her arms, and caress her, comfort her. It's all right, darling. Lark about a bit. Have some fun. Go on. It's allowed.

Vinny's mobile beeped behind her in the house. She jumped up and ran to answer it.

Catherine's voice was unusually flurried.

– Were you in bed? I know it's an hour later in France than here. But I thought you ought to know.

Vinny had to wrestle her mind around, back into the present. The standard lamp burnt very bright. Moths clattered against the shade. She flinched back, away from their fat furry bodies and propeller wings.

– Adam's had an accident, Catherine said: earlier this evening. Don't laugh. He fell into the river.

Adam had been taken by ambulance to Bart's, where he was staying overnight, recovering from having swallowed a lot of Thames water and Thames mud, being tested for waterborne diseases. Catherine had just got home, having been allowed to remain with him until late.

– He was pissed, she said: fooling about. That's all. He'll be fine. Don't worry.

Vinny's mind seized up.

– What about you? Are you all right? she asked.

– I suppose so, Catherine said: I don't know really.

Vinny paused, listening to both of them breathing.

– Actually I'm terribly fed up with everything, Catherine said: I'd like to talk to you about it. But not tonight. I'm too shattered. I'll ring you tomorrow.

Late next morning Vinny went back to visit Jeanne and Lucien. Over an aperitif she reported the news of Adam falling into the river. They listened to this second instalment of the story with calm; a certain pleasure.

They were used to strange happenings. Over the years they had revealed to her the existence of witches and wizards in surrounding villages, still believed by some to help with everything from love affairs to childbirth. They had recounted the local legends of the Devil's Table in the forest, of the human sacrifices supposedly once performed there. Vinny knew her probing for details was touristic bad manners, but she had persevered nonetheless. Lucien told her, grinning, that the rumours of diabolical influence up on the hillsides functioned to make safe love nests among the boulders for the local youngsters to do their summer court-ing in. What else did she expect? Robert had been seen taking girls up there from time to time, years ago. People didn't approve of that: he had plenty of space at home, surely. Lucien showed her the caves outside his house, opening out of the granite cliff. Yes, of course, these lead to tunnels that go all through the forest, underneath it, and eventually join up with the crypt of the village church. They were used in the wars of religion, and again in the Revolution. Priests holed up in the fortified church and felt safe, because they knew they had an escape route. Jeanne was even more matter-of-fact. Those tunnels are all sealed up now, you can't explore them, and the caves are full of grass-snakes. If I see one I beat it to death with my stick.

Vinny slept well. No dreams of snakes. No ghosts. She had breakfast in the garden. The house was so clean she felt it ought not to be disturbed. She crept across the shining floor of the kitchen, erupted on to the steps. She wandered about outside with her cup of coffee, trampling down the grass to make herself a little space for sitting in. She perched in a deckchair, looking at the heap of rubbish she had piled out-side one of the sheds. She would build a bonfire later on and burn it.

She wanted to take some time off, go for a drive perhaps, but Catherine, in her phone call early that morning, had warned her to expect a visitor. Charlie would be arriving some time today with a rented van to pick up all Robert's paintings and take them back to London.

– But I was going to photograph them for you, Vinny said: won't that do?

– He says he's got to see the real thing, Catherine said: he's really impatient to see all the work. Just let him get on with it.

– OK, Vinny said.

– When everything's sorted out, Catherine said: a bit later on in the summer, I've decided that I'm going to go to India. Perhaps meet up with the boys. I need some time away. Would you like to come with me?

– Oh Cath, Vinny said.

If you haven't got enough money for the airfare I could pay for you, Catherine said.

– I'm not travelling on the proceeds of your novellas, thanks, Vinny said: if I come I'll pay for myself.

– Think about it, Catherine said.

Charlie phoned in the early afternoon, asking for directions from Sainte-Madeleine.

– I'm staying at the hotel in Sainte-Marthe. Is it all right if I come over right now?

They found the shed key eventually, in the most obvious place, hung on a nail just inside the back door. They unlocked the shed and took turns bringing the paintings out to show each other. First Vinny sat on the step while Charlie paraded canvases past her. Then they swapped round. He sat down to watch and she carried the next few pictures, one by one, up and down the path.

Some of the paintings were so large you had to hold them

from behind, by their cross-bars. The flat surfaces went sliding along, walked by a pair of feet sticking out underneath. They came alive, because they were such large, simplified, bright images, and because they were moving against the backdrop of lush greenery. Like a slide show going sideways, scarlet and crimson and flesh-colour flashing strobe-like in this May garden of green speckled with white.

Their perspective was unsettling. Two and three dimensions both at once. Drew you in then rebuffed you. You felt you had your nose flattened against someone's skin, and yet the treatment of the surface, chilly and flat, meant you were pushed away, kept distant; at the same time. Some of the reds, in the nude studies, made you think of wounds, of a body that's been stabbed.

This first group of pictures was all about flesh. Seen one by one they represented a dismemberment. A hand. A foot. A cunt. An eye. Put together they made one reassembled body. Flesh admired and longed for, caressed and gratified; flesh that forbade, repulsed and punished; that was bruised and scratched; pitied.

The second group was strongly narrative. These paintings employed props and costumes, as in some nineteenth-century allegorical drama. At first glance the pictures were so pastiched as to be hopelessly old-fashioned. Then you saw that the handling of the paint did make the work modern.

Robert had repeatedly painted a figure with Catherine's face, in imaginary landscapes of jungles and forests; in imaginary roles, as a goddess, a madonna, a bride. She was veiled in gauze; crowned with poppies; carried wreaths of lilies. She was unsmiling; evoked the harsh beauty of a Frida Kahlo self-portrait.

He had represented Vinny in a short, tight skirt, posed in urban settings of junkyards and derelict factories, dwarfed by huge bleak skies. Hands on hips, feet apart. Legs braced in high heels. Gangster's moll; tart; cigarette in her mouth. This one couldn't feel anything; carapace of muscles and makeup; she was like an alien. Her hard gaze attacked you: how much?

– Thanks a lot, Robert, Vinny said.

– Not exactly cutting edge, are they? Charlie said: that nude portrait in London of your sister's the best of the lot.

– You know it's Catherine? Vinny asked: did she tell you?

– Never said a word, Charlie said: but the minute I saw it I knew. It's obvious, if you've got eyes in your head.

– So what about the show? Vinny asked.

– We'll see, Charlie said: these will sell, for sure. If that's what you're asking.

Vinny helped Charlie load the paintings into the van. Then they built a bonfire and burned the rubbish from the pile outside the shed. Ancient newspapers, worm-eaten picture-frames, old boxes and broken furniture formed a sub-stantial pyre. They set aside the sacks of old porn mags, old sex manuals they found at the back of the paintings-store: someone might make something of them one day. They stood around the flames, poking them with pitchforks. Vinny cremated Robert anew. She collected up all his dis-membered parts, all his worn-out, cut-up bits, fed them into

288

these flames. Alchemy. To release him and say farewell. So that mourning could be properly done, and end, and his imaginary gold body could arise.

She was tired out. She sat down on the grass and yawned.

– D'you want to eat something? Charlie asked: I bought some food on the way here. I'll make us supper if you like.

Jeanne and Lucien arrived from shutting up their poultry. Wrapped in coats against the chill of the May night the four of them sat by the heaped red embers. Waiting for the lamb chops to grill they opened one of the bottles of claret Charlie had brought with him and clinked glasses. The moon rose, salmon-pink in the indigo sky, Venus at its heel. The stars came out.

PART SEVENTEEN

Arthur says I was ill for a long time, *cher* Monsieur; that my mind wandered sadly. I don't call it illness; rather, an adventure. My mind wandered to France and back. My mind wandered to Brussels and still does. But this is the last time I shall write to you, my dear master. From henceforth I shall keep my stories, my parcels of words, for myself. No more giving everything away: letters squandered to the flames. I shall keep my writing and not burn it and see, instead, what I can make of it.

I'll write no more to you, dear friend. But I'll write another novel; and perhaps you will read it in translation some day.

Do you remember how bitterly I complained before that I had nowhere to write? Now that I've returned, I've made myself a study. I've found myself a retreat for writing in. Outside.

In front of the house, *cher* Monsieur, we tend what you'd call the *jardin d'ornement*: a strip of grass edged with flower-beds. Behind the house, the garden slopes up to a hawthorn hedge. This marks the boundary of the cultivated part: beyond, the hill rears up towards the moor. The back garden is laid out on three narrow terraces, stepped steeply one above the other. The first is merely a grassy path where we hang the washing out to dry on a line between two apple trees, so that it can't be seen from the churchyard or the church. To witness the vicar's long woollen underpants, however clean, however neatly mended, flapping in the breeze, would offend the parishioners' sensibilities, apparently; distract them from their prayers. The second garden-step, or terrace, is set with fruit bushes and rows of vegetables, and a line of pear trees; and the third, and highest, is planted with apple trees, shrubs and flowers to make a kind of alley. Much too narrow for someone as tall and big as Arthur to pace along in comfort. But I like slipping in here between the glossy green leaves of the bay, the orange-blossom, the crab-apple.

If you sit here and wait quietly you see hedgehogs, dormice and voles going about their business. Thrushes, blackbirds, robins, chaffinches and sparrows dart to and fro. When it rains, the slugs and snails come out. None of them minds me. I'm just another animal; on two legs.

Here I have pitched my camp. I brought up two old sheets from the house, so patched and darned they are fit only for making rags, and tied them to the branches of a lilac bush on one side and then round to the hawthorn hedge. I weighted them on the ground with stones. Two sides of a pavilion to screen the parsonage below from my view. I've laid down a piece of old blue carpet for floor. Silky on my bare soles once I peel my stockings off. It marks out my space on the dry earth. Also I've carried up the wicker table and armchair from the outhouse, two cushions, my little desk, a basket of books, a bottle of water, a tin cup.

Soft walls of white construct my temporary house, billow in the warm wind, enclose me like wings. Overhead there's a green canopy studded with small apples as red as enamel beads, and to my left a screen of tall ferns with the sunlight dappling through them. Far above me are the moors, and the blue hills.

No-one can see me from the parsonage. Anyone climbing the crags and looking down might remark two sheets blowing in the wind and think nothing of it. So what? The vicar's laundry. But these aren't the sheets off our bed. They're the ones from childhood, that Emily and I slept in until they wore out, and then wore out again from being mended so much. Now, the light pierces them; they're like very old paper, almost transparent, and the waving shadows of the ferns dance over them like writing.